I0598025

MAIL
ORDER
BRIDE

MAIL ORDER BRIDE

A Western Tale of Love and Fate

Leo Du Lac

SUNSTONE
PRESS

SANTA FE

This book is entirely fictional and may contain views, opinions, premises, depictions, and statements by the author that are not necessarily shared or endorsed by Sunstone Press. The events, people, and incidents in this story are the sole product of the author's imagination. The story is fictional and any resemblance to individuals living or dead is purely coincidental. Sunstone Press assumes no responsibility or liability for the author's views, opinions, premises, depictions and statements in this book.

© 2009 by Leo Du Lac. All Rights Reserved.

No part of this book may be reproduced in any form or by any electronic or mechanical means including information storage and retrieval systems without permission in writing from the publisher, except by a reviewer who may quote brief passages in a review.

Sunstone books may be purchased for educational, business, or sales promotional use. For information please write: Special Markets Department, Sunstone Press, P.O. Box 2321, Santa Fe, New Mexico 87504-2321.

Book design ▷ Vicki Ahl
Body typeface ▷ Antique Olive ◇ Display typeface ▷ Caflisch Script Pro
Printed on acid free paper

Library of Congress Cataloging-in-Publication Data

Du Lac, Leo.
 Mail order bride : a western tale of love and fate / by Leo Du Lac.
   p. cm.
 ISBN 978-0-86534-718-2 (softcover : alk. paper)
 1. Arizona–Fiction. I. Title.
 PS3604.U22M35 2009
 813'.6–dc22

                    2009014733

WWW.SUNSTONEPRESS.COM
SUNSTONE PRESS / POST OFFICE BOX 2321 / SANTA FE, NM 87504-2321 /USA
(505) 988-4418 / ORDERS ONLY (800) 243-5644 / FAX (505) 988-1025

1

Nearly every Saturday afternoon, Buck Garett would saddle Prince on his brother's toil-infested ranch and head out across the darkening desert to visit Zulinda's Cantina—the only one in the little town of Las Collinas, in the wide-open spaces of the Arizona Territory.

There were twenty-seven Mexicans in Las Colinas and one American who handled the trading post. But the hospitable Zulinda had the place of entertainment. On one such night, Buck Garett, after having his usual number of two bit drinks, drowsily slumped against the bar while he watched Zulinda's every move. She was the only woman in the Territory who would share her bed with him, but he didn't like the way she flirted with all the drunks lined up against the bar.

Still young enough appearing and vigorous for his forty years, Garett was beginning to dislike his wayward years, wondering if Zulinda was really the only one meant for him, or was he just getting lonely for a woman of his own whom he could love.

He didn't like the lot of gringos that hung around the cantina; any one would have cut his throat, but for Zulinda. She stood up for him, and sometimes went against her greaser friends, as she called them. Buck had little more than hate for the lot, but he seldom had an outright brawl.

Garett was ranch foreman for his brother, in that there was gnawing resentment. His brother owned a vast 80,000 acres of barrel cactus and bunch grass, overrun more than not by Apache. But there was real loyalty between the two of them. Buck Garett would never betray his brother, nor would Buck ever tell his brother that he was married to the only woman he had ever looked up to, Elena Montez. When Garett went west to buy into his brother's ranch, he rescued Elena from the Apaches instead, for which he spent his fortune.

But even Elena didn't know that Buck Garett was still in love with her. At the time Garett didn't know Elena from Eve. Why did he do it?

As Garett drove by Mission San Xavier del Bac, his fortune loaded onto his wagon, the padre took Garett in and fed him. That night, after a long needed bath, Garett slept in a clean bed. The padre decided that Garett was as brave as he boasted and had grit. He told Garett about Elena Montez, but it wasn't until the next morning, while Garett was watering his team at the tank, ready to leave, when the padre said, "Mister Garett, if you want to do something good for the world, you would rescue Elena Montez. She was taken from the Mission fields while gathering beans. That was six weeks ago." The padre was a talker; he had tears in his eyes, running down his cheeks. "Six weeks."

Garett was taken in by what the padre had to say, and he never regretted what he had done, even when Elena became his brother's wife.

The next week, Garett appeared at the cantina. There he met his friend Nido, one of the few Mexicans he could abide. When Nido came into the cantina, Garett got up and the two took a table in a corner away from the boisterous crew. Garett would say at the cantina things that he would never say when he was sober. Garett looked up to Nido. Nido meant neat in Mexican, and Nido had sense to marry one of the few girls around and settle down. Garett respected Nido and his opinions. He had an education after a fashion, read both Spanish and English. He was tall and sported an ample moustache that needed trimming every week. Garett had a moustache, but it never got the care it needed. Nido had class, and he was faithful to his wife. Which was saying a lot for him.

Garett talked and laughed when he was sober, but he wasn't really happy. He liked to talk and laugh with Nido and at the same time watch Zulinda's every move and wonder, yet again, if she was really meant for him. But he knew better. When he crawled in bed with her, after he went to sleep she went to a different room and another dollar from one of her greaser friends.

There was derision and scorn in the word greaser. Buck Garett seldom used the word openly. But he had a like feeling for his brother when he spoke of his wife. "Elena was the best investment he ever made." He meant that because of his half treaty with Marques Colorado, the Apache chief: eleven cows every winter to leave them alone. Buck Garett had bargained for the release of Elena from captivity. His brother had forgotten that the trade had been Buck's and the treaty meant nothing to the Indians, just an empty promise. Buck Garett was the one who had made the investment. At a sign from Nido, Zulinda bought a round of drinks. He put four bits on the table, which Zulinda picked up while brushing her arm against Buck, so he would remember her anew. Buck allowed her a half smile and she rubbed her hand against his neck to let him know that she would be around after closing the cantina; she wanted the dollar. The dark faces at the bar stared in Buck's direction, any one of them would have shot him in the back, but Zulinda would not have allowed it. Buck Garett, the bachelor, became accustomed to that. They were all sure that Zulinda gave each her individual attention. She only catered to the American because he had money. They could tolerate that, she was their bitch.

After Zulinda sashayed back to the bar, Nido picked up his glass. "Here's mud in your eye," he laughed. He liked that kind of toast when drinking with Buck. He had learned it from him. It expressed his feeling for the people who had taken over his country, but he knew it was futile to go beyond that.

Nido was in his mid-thirties and had little ones to grace his three room adobe cabin. Without Nido the population of Las Collinas would drop to twenty. People looked up to him; he was a reading man. He was also a business man, ready to resolve anyone's problems for a buck. He supported his family well. Buck said that, because Nido had gouged many a peso out of him. Buck hardly resented that, because he was as likable a greaser as any vaquero he had ever ridden with.

It is time that you should know where the word greaser came from. Buck was in California after he rescued Elena. That was when his brother married Elena fair and square, after Buck ran away escorting a wagon train to California, leaving no forward address. There in California, they have these Mexican carts, carretas, wooden wheels and axles. When they travel down the road the wheels squeak like hell and the natives walk along applying soap or tallow to the axles, hence greaser. The word has been in use long enough that it is no longer uncomplimentary, but Buck didn't use it often, except when he was mad at someone, who might stick a knife in his gut the first chance he got.

They clinked glasses again, and Nido wished Buck good health that time. Buck was drunk, he spilled half his drink and blurted out, "I'm tired of sharing that bitch with all those greasers. I need a woman of my own." Garett gestured toward the sorry lot, their attention on Zulinda leaning against the crumbling wall, her sagging breasts outlined in the folds of her one piece dress.

Garett was more than a common cowhand. There was money in back of him after a fashion. That was why his best friend, for a few pesos took advantage of him, after he had a few drinks.

"Why you not take one of our fine Mexican girls. I have one in mind for you." Nido spoke with pride and enthusiasm. It was business with Nido, the way he made his living.

Buck couldn't think of one unmarried girl in the area, but he was a little drunk.

"When she have a few more years—I arrange for you—for a few pesos, of course."

"You old bastard, you'd take money from your grandmother for doing her a favor."

Nido's black eyes opened wide, edging onto resentment. Nido needed a friend or some one with money; he knew best how to wheedle it out of Buck when he was drunk.

"Hell, I'm a grown man. I don't need a kid around the house." That ended the tension, but Buck knew that Nido had something up his sleeve. Buck laughed, his mouth big and wide. "You can read English?"

Nido pulled a folded ad from his pocket and waved it in front of Buck. Buck had his pride. He wasn't going to allow Nido to pull anything on him. Nido spread the newspaper out on the table and pointed.

Buck turned the paper around several times before he got it right side up. Buck was wondering if Nido had lied to him, or had he just forgotten how to read English. Buck nudged closer to the candle and from lack of practice, he drawled, "Graduate nurse will consider marriage to well-to-do rancher. Please write for details."

Buck's supposed friend grinned from ear to ear, while Buck gawked at him. With his dark hands he twisted and stretched his ample moustache. Buck was sure he had read the ad several times to get the true meaning.

Nido was all business and stuck his newly preened mustache close to Buck's face. "What you think? Nurse, she make fine wife."

Nido was eager as hell to make a buck.

"Who in hell ever heard of ordering a wife?" Buck asked.

"They do it all the time—men go west leave women home. Some have adventurous spirit—like to go west. Why I need to write for you."

Nido's eager smile was hidden by his black mustache. He took a swallow of whiskey to help withstand the suspense. Nido could see something good in the venture. He would be the instrument bringing two people together. He seemed imbued with a sneaky streak of romanticism and would go home and tell his wife and she would be happy for him and they would lay naked in bed and talk and play.

Nido was proud of the education he had acquired haphazardly; it gave him the feeling of esteem he needed. He loathed hard work and saved himself for his wife and kids. There would soon be seven. That would boost the population of Los Collinas to twenty-nine. Buck was envious of him and his family and the way he lived in the wild territory.

"You want for me to write for you one bride, maybe two." Nido gave a chuckle, hoping to cinch the deal.

"Hell, one woman is enough."

"It would be worth twenty pesos. One woman."

Buck's mind was foggy. He didn't take Nido seriously. He was only biding his time until Zulinda closed the cantina and he could go up to her room.

"Then it settle. Write for you one wife by mail out of Chicago."

Absentmindedly, Buck put his head on the table to catch fifty winks.

When business closed down, Zulinda went to Buck's table and brushed her broad hips against his thighs to wake him up. Buck opened one eye then the other. Nido was gone. Zulinda picked up the glasses while smiling at him. There was enough rapport between the two that she resented new customers. Buck put his arm around her waist to let her know that he felt something for her. He kept his feeling for her greasers to himself; it was because of them that he knew there could never be anything between Garett and Zulinda.

Feeling like hell, Buck reached in his pocket for a chaw of tobacco. The plug was gone. When he felt a little closer he discovered some Mexican coins were missing and two silver dollars. Buck supposed that was a down payment on the deal he had made. That would feed Nido's wife and kids for a couple of weeks. He couldn't begrudge Nido the money. He probably needed it.

Zulinda came back and blew out the last flickering candle in the already dark room. The last Mexican wove by and Buck staggered out to Prince, watered him at the tank and looked up to Zulinda's room. There was a light and Buck knew she was waiting for him, but Nido had taken his last dollar.

The night was wasted. Buck rode back to the ranch by the light of the moon. Near the house he drove Prince through a pond to freshen up a bit. It was just getting light when he walked into the mess room where the cook was boiling coffee in his huge granite pot.

"Hi Josh." Buck then mumbled something to him in Mexican and poured himself a cup of coffee. Josh needed a shave as usual. He was old and settled on the ranch where there would be plenty of food to the last. Still, he was skinny as a rail. Because of his whiskers, Buck couldn't see many wrinkles, but he surmised he was old, the way he took short steps and puttered about. He cooked plenty of steaks and beans, no one could complain. After Buck had eaten, he hung up his wet clothes in the bunk house and had a few winks of sleep.

Later that morning while he was riding the range, he noticed the first signs of spring. He got down from a fresh horse and cut out the tongue of a prickly pear. A bright yellow flower had burst forth from the top edge of the tongue. The flower had a slight streak of red on one of the pedals. He took the flower back to the house and placed it on the crudely hewn oak table in the dining room.

It was always cool inside the thick walls of the adobe structure when the sun was blistering the ground outside. The walls, once brushed over with lime were peeling, but Elena kept the house clean, even the floors of solid packed clay were swept clean.

Elena came in to greet Buck. He had always liked her smile, and wondered if that was what kept him from forgetting her after she married his brother. He only wished the smile were really meant for him. "Hello Buck." Her voice was sincere, but Buck knew she didn't give him the least encouragement, nor did he expect it. He had lost her fair and square; he was resigned. It had been his fault, but there was a magic sparkle felt when around her and it never went away. Elena took the flower, put it in a red pottery dish with water and placed it on a nitch in the adobe wall in front of a painting of the Lady of Guadalupe.

"The water will bring the flower back to life."

Nourished by the moisture in the cactus tongue, the flower hadn't wilted in the slightest, and in water it would flower for days.

With his slouch black hat in his hand, Buck stood there trying not to admire Elena. Buck was afraid he might let her know by his actions that he had always hoped he meant something to her and since they were both awkward together, he was afraid he would spoil it.

Garett had driven right into the Apache camp with his supplies loaded onto the wagon, a little canvas over the top against the wind and rain. He showed the Indians he was not afraid. As the chief looked over his belongings, Buck demanded Elena in exchange. As said before, he didn't know Elena from Eve. Marques could have given him any one of his misfits and Buck would have never known the difference. They had Elena hidden away in one of the tepees. After Marques examined the trade goods, he sent for her.

Elena had already settled in her Indian way of life in one of the wickiup. She stood there like a wild animal looking up at Buck, pitifully frightened, wondering if her new fate could be worse than living with the Apache. She had on very little clothes, a dress of cheap material that came to her knees, no hat, no shoes, and it was cloudy and cold that time of the day. After the exchange, she still hesitated getting into the wagon. Buck knew she needed assurance, so he said, "The padre sent me." She climbed in. Buck still had a few blankets left and he wrapped one around Elena, just as Marques' oldest son came along.

He was harder to deal with than the chief himself. Garett had already completed the deal, but the young chief was determined to have the rest of the covering. Buck was intent on saving a few blankets, but the arrogant young man lifted them out of the wagon one at a time and handed them to the Indian women. The last one Buck had draped around Elena. He grabbed it and wrapped it around himself. That was the last of the store bought clothes; they ignored the buffalo hide thrown over the wagon seat.

Garett had anticipated the worst and had slipped on an extra pair of trousers and two extra jackets. After they left the village and had dropped over the first knoll, Buck stopped the team and took off one pair of pants and two jackets. Elena put them on and laughed for the first time; Buck knew then in rescuing her, that he had done mankind a great service. That night, Elena and Buck slept close together in the wagon with plenty of long grass on the floor, covered with the buffalo robe draped over the two of them.

Buck's brother was married to Maryanne at the time and Elena only stayed two days, and then asked to be taken back to the mission. She was much older than the Indians and Mexican girls boarding there, but she fitted in helping the younger ones to adjust.

When John's wife was shot in the back by a renegade Apache, Elena left the mission to take charge of the house. She brought

John out of his grief and finally at his request, Elena married him. She was never a common law wife. She had one of the itinerant Padres do it up the right way.

Garett should have married Elena at the time; by now he was sure that she would have expected it of him. But Marques Colorado had told him of gold in the hills to the west; he was only trying to get the whites to move out of his territory. But Garett had hightailed it west, trying to recover his fortunes. When Garett found that Marques had duped him, he led a lost wagon train on to California. Buck had never been a winning man and that was the worst mistake he ever made.

Meanwhile, he didn't want to make a fool out of himself in front of his brother's wife, so he was glad when she chided, "When was the last time you had a bath, Buck?" She stood there, neat and slender in her long black dress, her cascading hair covered with a white lace mantilla.

"On the way home last night, I drove Prince through a pond." He ran his hand across his throat to indicate the depth of the water. "When I jumped off the water was all the way up to my neck—plenty of water for the cattle for a while."

Elena knew about the rains. The ceiling was still dripping from a few low spots in the earth covering above.

Sunday was another long dull day. Buck didn't know it, but it was just the lull before a storm. The vaqueros had reported the Apaches on the move south. Marques Colorado, long time friend of the whites, was among those on the war path. He had been up to his tricks again; when miners became too numerous, he again told them of gold finds further west in the Colorado hills. Buck hadn't taken it amiss, when Marques Colorado told him of the great gold finds.

But a group of brawlers didn't take kindly to the chief's misinformation. They tied him to a tree and beat him until he couldn't stand. When they released him he slid to the ground and crawled away. Now he sided with his son-in-law Cochise, an outlaw in his own right. There would be no rest for the wagon trains going west that summer.

While Buck had been away on his search for gold, John's wife had been killed and that's when he married Elena.

Elena was staring at Buck. She hadn't intended to. She had never thanked him for having saved her from Marques Colorado. He had at one time hoped she would do that through marriage; but Buck had fouled that up, but good.

Elena was slender from work. She had brought seeds from the mission and in season she planted a garden and carried water to make it grow. In her black dress, which she wore for the most part, she looked mature and wholesome. Her eyes were dark and far apart and she had high cheekbones from her Indian heritage, but there was always a freshness in her face. Her hollow cheeks didn't distract from her wholesomeness. They only accented the beauty of her full red lips. She had lived the dregs, but with her smattering of education at the mission and determination she had become a well-bred frontier wife.

Buck felt self-conscious standing there. He could never become indifferent to Elena and he was sure she was aware of that. He put on his distorted, black, felt hat and walked out. Both were glad the meeting was over.

The sun had already warmed the earth. By midday it would be hot. Buck Garett climbed up on the roof to relieve Ferd. He was stretched out on the dirt floor, tired from the long and boring night watch. They could never relax their guard. Marques was coming.

Buck liked the wrinkled old Ferd. If there was ever a Mexican he liked better he didn't know who it was. Buck would send him down to eat plenty of tortillas and coffee. Buck gave Ferd a little nudge with his boot to let him know he was there to take his place. Ferd was asleep, wrapped in his ample serape.

Buck leaned over the parapet wall to scan the brush for any sneaky Apache. Some were just curious how the whites lived. But some would put an arrow through a lone man without giving it a second thought. Buck picked up the telescope that went with the watch. Heat waves danced in the air. The lime that covered the adobe was soft; it brushed off onto his dirty clothes, leaving them a sickening white. The numerous coats had peeled in places, creating a mottled effect of blotches, but there were enough white coats on the wall to blind one in the afternoon sun.

The roof was supported by juniper poles that lay on the adobe walls, yet there wasn't a tree in sight. They were all dragged in from distant hills. Brush was thrown over the timbers, then hay and layers of sod, which had settled over the years to match the barren earth.

Juniper poles had been set in the ground to form an enclosure around the house that included a barn, the mess house and a few outbuildings, and a dug well of some sorts. Windmills were still new in the west, but John tried to imitate things he had read in a book. It pumped water after a fashion if he kept it patched up. Inside the fence, dirt had been piled against the poles to give added height to a wall as a protection to the vaqueros when attacked by the Apaches.

2

 $\mathcal{A}$s weeks dragged by, Buck forgot about the letter Nido was supposed to have written. One Saturday while he was biding his time at the cantina, the Mexicans were friendlier to Buck than usual, but Zulinda acted as if he had betrayed her. After a third drink, Buck could stand the suspense no longer and he asked right out, "What is the matter with you Zulinda. You act as if I am no longer your friend."

"I heerd you ordered a wife out of Chicago. I didn't know you could do that—and I don't even know where Chicago is." She pouted pitifully, like a child. Buck didn't think that he meant that much to her.

Buck tried to reassure her. "Oh I'd never do a thing like that." Buck had no idea that Nido had actually sent the letter. But Zulinda was uppity, as if Buck was the only man in her life and he had run out on her. Buck wanted to take her seriously, but he got to thinking, any one of the Mexicans would be better than he. If she really wanted to get serious with one man.

Nido came in acting high and mighty, 'cause he was a reading man. He stood there glaring at Buck. "You owe me the price of a stamp."

"Stamp." A joke was a joke, but Nido was overstepping his bounds. Buck hit him a glancing blow on the cheek. "Right is right." Buck didn't want to fight unless he was right and had a good reason. Nido ducked Buck's second blow and wouldn't fight back.

"You order me to write that letter." He grinned, causing his mustache to curl up, and then he felt his jaw. "I mail that letter weeks ago, just like you asked me to."

Buck was itching to hit Nido again, but he never beat up on anyone who wouldn't defend himself. Nido was no coward. He had saved Buck's life once, when he shot an Apache from his pony using his thirteen-pound, dog-eared rifle—that was the accomplishment.

Soon the cantina was crowded and everyone laughing at Buck and the letter. Two Mexicans went over and hugged him, glad Buck would no longer be in the running for Zulinda's affections. But he was careful that neither stuck a knife into his gut. Both the Mexicans and Indians resented whites; their territory had been taken over recently by the Americans. There were minor revolts. Not all had buckled down by the new rule, but things were beginning to shape up, since a number of the perpetrators had been hanged for murdering Governor Bent's family while he tried to defend them.

Everyone was happy and bought a round of drinks. Only Zulinda acted cold and pouted. When Buck and Nido went to a corner table, Nido took Zulinda aside and explained. "Buck really do need a woman of his own. I don't know any other way except to let one grow up. But, Buck at hees age, he don't need a kid in the house."

Zulinda tried to smile, but couldn't. She didn't brush up against Buck with her big hips all evening. Buck didn't think it would be long before she was herself again, 'cause he never expected a reply from the letter. It was Nido's way of getting a few bucks of support for his family. Buck never begrudged him of that.

"Eff this deal go through, you still owe me forty-eight pesos." Then Buck knew that he had rifled his pockets of two silver dollars. Buck knew silver dollars were worth several pesos. Buck didn't want to argue the difference, so he tried to forget all about it. Nido never mentioned taking the chewing tobacco, but Buck knew he had.

Weeks later Buck went to the trading post with the wagon to bring back flour for tortillas. The damn cook always made tortillas until Buck never knew what a loaf of bread looked like. But he had to eat. He was thin at one hundred and seventy, so he didn't want to get any thinner. He needed that weight for an unexpected tussle with an Apache who might sneak up on him at any time. They moved with the sun and the sun was always moving.

Grover as Buck said was the only non-Mexican in town and he ran the trading post. It consisted of the store, wagon yard, corral and black smith shop. He was a skinny sneaky old bastard. He winked and whistled at Buck as he handed him the letter from Chicago. The way he looked at Buck, Buck knew he had read what was in it. Buck had never read a letter before. He was so overcome with this unexpected event that he added a bottle of whiskey to the grocery list, along with lye for making soap.

He didn't stop to see Zulinda; if a man was to take a wife, he had to become respectable. After he was down the trail a piece with the team, Buck took a big drink from the bottle before he opened the letter and another after he read it. She was a coming and Buck didn't know what to do.

Buck moped around the ranch until Elena felt sorry for him. "What's ailing you Buck? Is it the spring fever? Could I fix you some sassafras tea?"

"No. I don't want any tea, but I could use another bottle of whiskey."

Later that day Elena washed Buck's dirty trousers and didn't even ask him to carry the water. That was when she discovered the letter in a pocket of his trousers. She spread it out on a log in front of the fireplace to dry. There was no privacy in the house as far as John was concerned. When he came in for supper he saw the letter. The ink had faded in the washing. But they made out the most important parts.

Dear Buck,

I was overcome by your romantic proposal of marriage. You write that I will be your very beloved forever. I had other proposals, but yours was the most romantic. I like the fact that you know Spanish as well as English. I take it that you are well educated and at the same time very modest. I will be on the stage that goes through Tucson between the fifteenth and the twentieth of June.

Buck was glad that the rest of the letter was so smudged from the washing that John couldn't read any more.

Buck ate for the most part with the ranch hands, but that evening, he was invited to the main house. That was a real occasion. The table was set with white tallow candles and the room in lamplight. John and his son Jewell were already seated when Buck arrived. Jewell was from his first wife, Maryanne. He was eighteen, a blond kid. John babied Jewell, afraid he might get killed by the Indians like his mom did. But the boy knew how to handle a gun and went often on his own to shoot rabbits.

He sat there quiet like and mannerly, minding his own business. He and Buck had a good relationship; he kinda looked up to Buck. Buck taught him more of the real west than his Pa ever would.

They were eating Mexican style, the meat chopped in little pieces with tortillas, not tough at all like the steaks at the mess house. Everyone was quiet looking holes through Buck, expecting him to broach the subject of the Carver girl out of Chicago. He knew Elena was especially disturbed, thinking of another woman in the house. Her hands shook as she placed the desert on the table.

John could stand it no longer. "What is this forthcoming marriage we hear about?" he asked bluntly. That was just the way he was. Big, getting fat and his face furred with wrinkles from the heat and wind. His hair was graying but it was hard to tell, his hair was blond. Buck's hair was black, and he had only a grey hair or two in his head.

Buck looked over to Elena; he shouldn't have because she never talked about her life as a slave with the Apache. Buck realized he was responsible for the new girl. He felt sick.

Elena then asked, "Who ees thees girl anyway? Deed you know her before?"

"Some old biddy from Chicago—if you must know—she be a mail-order-bride. The scribe wrote the letter for me."

The three looked at each other and Buck wanted to skink through the dirt floor.

But Elena eased the tension. "Maybe thees the best thing could happen to you, Buck. Now you never get drunk again."

Jewell stopped eating his desert and was about to laugh at Elena's remark, but one look in her direction and his face sobered. "I'm glad it didn't happen to me." There was pity in his remark, as though Buck had been struck down by the plague.

"Her name be Suzy Carver; probably couldn't get a husband in Chicago so she advertised."

There was a long silence as the family seemed too astonished to speak, their eyes staring at Buck. Things were moving too fast.

Buck poured coffee from his cup into his saucer and started to blow on it, then drank noisily. Elena was annoyed; she was always trying to break Buck of the strange ways he had acquired during his wanderings. "Buck, do you intend to drink coffee like that after you're married?"

Buck stopped drinking long enough to reply, "Why not? I've done it all my life."

"Why don't you let his new wife train him some manners?" John glared at his wife.

John had aged since he lost Maryanne. But he could still scream when things didn't go the way he liked; Buck didn't want any of that tonight.

Buck was stunned at the thought of changing his ways. He didn't think the Carver girl was any of their business. Buck lost his appetite and stopped eating. The tone in John's voice seemed to indicate Buck didn't have the right to get married, but Buck was hoping his brother didn't really mean it that way. Buck didn't think he would have anything very intelligent to say about Suzy Carver, so he hadn't brought up the subject. Now he knew exactly why he had been invited to supper.

Suddenly, Jewell came to life, smiling in Buck's direction. "Wow! Uncle Buck getting married!" He roared with laughter, poking fun at Buck. This was about the last straw. Buck could have held it against Jewell, but he felt about the same himself.

Elena was pouring coffee to occupy her time; her dark hair was done up in a swirl on the top of her head and held there by two sharp wooden pins. She generally left the disciplining of her stepson to his father, but she looked sternly at the kid until he shut his mouth and started to bolt his dessert.

Elena still had the coffee pot in her hand as she held her head high and in a queenly fashion announced, "No one is going to make fun of Buck. Marriage is a sacred contract." Buck recalled how she frequently brought up her brief few months of book learning and religious training at the mission. She expressed it sincerely to prevent botching things.

Jewell sobered up and stammered, "I didn't mean to laugh at Uncle Buck. It's just that I never thought of you getting married—ever."

John sat there taking it all in, but being Buck's brother, Buck knew he'd have his say and that would be the hardest blow. He always thought he had to guide Buck; but listening to the three of them, Buck was beginning to realize what he had gotten himself into.

Elena was all compliments. "It takes a lot of nerve to get married. It shows what you Garetts are made of." She sat down and started to eat her dessert. She looked over to her husband, waiting for what he had to add. Buck was expecting him to explode.

Buck's half-brother—that's what made him a lot older than Buck—looked as though he might be posing for a painting; such was his esteem for himself and his opinions. Buck could have used a little of that esteem right then himself. Buck knew his brother was boiling inside because of the way he had handled this proposed marriage contract.

"It takes nerve to get married, but it also takes a sense of responsibility." He started waving his hands at Buck and turned red in the face. Buck knew he was in for it. "Do you realize that girl is due on the next stage and the Apaches are plundering every wagon train along the trail—have been for weeks? You can see smoke from the hills in the north pasture right this minute."

John was at the head of the table, Elena at the foot and Buck and Jewell on either side. Elena beamed at Buck, she was only happy for him. "Oh, Buck, it will be so good to have another woman in the house, but you do have to make plans."

She got up and went around to her husband and put her arms around him in his high-backed chair. "You sound so angry—you don't want Buck to have a wife of his own?"

"Like hell I don't—the way he looks at you at times—I know what he's thinking, but I married you fair. The trouble with Buck, it takes him too long to make up his mind. He left you at the mission and went west, didn't he? He never said he was ever coming back."

John paused and asked Elena to sit down, and then he went on. But Buck butted in; he had to say something sensible. "I know my shortcomings; I'm not trying to be perfect." The three looked at each other as though they had known that all along.

Then John took the floor. "I'll bet that girl is out there right now surrounded by Marques Colorado and his braves. He used to be our ally—stood up against Cochise to keep him in check. Then those fur traders at the post beat him up 'cause he lied to them—then he went mad. He headed south again this year with his whole tribe to plunder. He's waiting for the Frenchman Du Lac—they got all his goods last year and he didn't have any better sense than to come again this year. She's on that stage—Buck, you're responsible for her life. You don't want her to go through the hell Elena did living with the Indians."

John looked at his wife; he was disgusted with his brother, but that wasn't difficult for him. Buck tried to take everything in a kindly way, but John was his half-brother and still thought he had to wipe Buck's nose.

They got up from the table and John put his hand on Buck's shoulder. He was taller than Buck and Buck felt he was trying to remind him he was still boss. Buck was just the foreman; Buck had spent his intended investment buying Elena back from the Indians.

"Tomorrow before sun up," John said, "we'll be on our way to find that coach. The Frenchman is due in the territory with a new caravan of trade goods any time now. We hope the stage had sense enough to join up with him."

They settled in the spacious parlor where a fire was burning in the hearth, laid with native stones that covered half the wall. The adobe walls were crumbling in places and Buck felt as though they were tumbling in on him, but the furniture was sturdy enough to support the walls even if they caved in. Then Buck began to feel more at ease, realizing everyone meant the best for him.

It was late when they had finished the plans for the next day. As Buck got up to go to the bunkhouse, Elena walked over and kissed him. "Good luck, Buck," and Buck felt out of place because it was his brother's wife, but any touch from her brought back regretful memories.

Miss Carver had written she would arrive between the

fifteenth and the twentieth of June, but Buck knew of no stage with a real schedule. There were a few fine weather coaches that stopped at cow towns and fleeted across the dry prairie like dust devils. It would soon be too blamed hot for the lackadaisical drivers, but there were always a number of unscheduled mud wagons.

3

*T*hey were ready to leave early the next morning. Elena, hair still hanging loose, had a light robe over her night clothes. Her whole attention was directed to John, astride his Indian pony, the stirrup straps adjusted for his long kegs. John was telling Elena goodbye. "Buck might be a little shy about marrying this girl, or he'd be married to you right now."

Buck didn't want to get into anything sentimental right then, but he knew it was all true. He mounted Prince and went on so he would not have to listen.

"After Maryanne was killed—your release brought a truce with Marques Colorado. I hope you won't hold it against me—because you turned out to be the best thing that ever happened to me."

Elena beamed as tears welled up in her eyes. "That is the nicest thing that you ever said to me, my husband." She reached up with her small hand and grabbed his huge fist.

"I should say something nice. This is going to be a battle to the end. I may not come back."

"Don't talk this way. You may jinx the outcome," Elena said solemnly.

John released her hand and she walked back toward the house, but when she saw Jewell, she turned and followed him.

No one had awakened him. He was still treated like a kid, even though he was a man. He went running, pulling his blue shirt over his head. He would never be the stature of his father. He was more like his mother.

"Pa, I want to go along," he shouted as he tucked his shirt in and slammed his hat onto his head.

"You are too young to fight Apaches."

"Tain't so. Buck kilt his first Apache long before he was my age."

Buck was back on the scene and John looked at Buck sternly. "Sorry. Guess I shouldn't have told him."

Jewell refused to take the matter lightly. He grabbed his felt hat and pounded the dust from his trousers. Elena tried to talk to him, but he refused to listen.

"We're not going to the trading post for supplies. We're taking the responsibility of grown men. You can take the responsibility of a grown man by guarding the ranch," John said sternly.

"Let someone else guard the ranch," Jewell shouted.

"We need someone around who's interested. If the Apache get wind that we pulled too many men from the ranch it might be more profitable to loot the ranch."

John always sounded angry. It seemed the best way to convince his son.

"I thought you had an agreement with Marques, ten or eleven cows every January," Elena said.

"The deal went off when he crossed our land to loot wagon

trains. Now you keep someone on that roof day and night," he said to Elena.

Elena walked over and put her arms around Jewell. He shook them off and looked at his father.

John ignored him.

Buck reined up Prince and they pulled out. Jewell threw his hat in the dirt and ran toward the house. John was right. He was acting like a baby. They didn't need any babies along.

John and Buck each had a telescope tucked in a rifle holster. They carried them along wherever they went. They had learned to use the scope to bring the enemy up close; by watching the Indians, they sometimes gained an advantage over them.

Buck rode along with his brother for about an hour, and then cut through the wilderness toward Las Collinas to pick up the scribe. "If he got me into this, and I was going to have to pay forty-eight pesos, he was going to earn every cent of it."

Buck took Marcos along, a dedicated Mexican, who would risk his life every day for a plate of beans and a few tortillas. He was heavy boned and lean. Buck guessed he weighed twelve pounds when he was born and had grown in proportion. He was dark and slow to move and dressed in a heavy leather jacket and chaps to protect his limbs from spiny brush. Marcos was all go; he never let up, and slept but a few hours at night. He generally wore a heavy mustache, but last night he shaved it off. His hair was long enough to braid; he had it cut once a year. Marcos had always talked of lassoing an Apache girl for a squaw-wife, but nothing had come of it but talk. If he really wanted an Indian wife, he could have bought one long ago.

It was midmorning, when the two arrived at Nido's crumbling adobe house, with a shingle over the door that read, ESCRIVE TAMBIEN ENGLES. He was telling the Americans in Spanish that he also wrote in English. Buck reined in, leaving the animal to munch a few twigs. Buck was at the bastard Nido's house. He had disturbed Buck's peaceful life. Buck strode up to the porch with a gun in hand

and kicked the door in. Marcos stayed with the horses.

Senor Nido was sitting at his desk writing a letter, getting some other damn fool into trouble. It was dark inside and Buck didn't know how he could see. There was but one window worth mentioning in the room, a transparent hide stretched over the opening. The scribe got a grim expression on his dark face as Buck stuck his gun into his ragged mustache. He half raised his hands and stood up, leaning away from the business end of the gun with disbelief in his eyes. "Buena manjana, amigo." He spoke first. In a tense situation a little flattery never hurt. Nido reached out to take Buck's hand in a gesture of friendship, but Buck struck it down.

"We are friends, you do not need zee gun," Nido said.

"I need the gun, cause I want you to get your hat on and come with me."

"We are frens—ol frens. We drink together; shake hans with your ol' fren." The bastard reached out and hit Buck's gun, knocked it on the bare earth and stepped on it. "Now you tell me what you want. Only a fren could take advantage of me; had it been one of those drunks that hang around Zulinda, he'd have been dead or me."

"I want you to come and help me rescue that mail order girl. I think she be surrounded by Apache."

He was more of a friend than Buck thought. "Why you not say so? I go gladly to help a pretty girl. But not at the point of a gun." Nido had his pride; he held his head high. Buck thought he was going to be mad at him, but before they reached the door, Nido picked up Buck's gun and handed it to him, handle first; then Buck knew that things were back to normal.

His wife, a chubby Mexican girl, had been hanging wash; she came around to the front door of the house with a baby on a board fastened to her back, Indian style. The children followed. When they found out their daddy was leaving, they swarmed all over him. His wife rubbed her face against his and the smaller children hung to his legs.

When Nido could break away, he said with pride, "There will be a woman in your house."

Buck was impatient; he knew what he was there for. But he had to admit, Nido had a nice family.

Marcos was fastening the cinch on Nido's saddle, when his oldest son came out the lopsided door with Nido's 13 pound dog-eared rifle. Nido could tell that the kick to the door hadn't helped it any.

As they mounted up, Nido was laughing, pleased with his abilities to write. "So the letter bring good results," he had to brag, but it irked Buck.

"Just think it out, "Buck said. "She be twenty and I be forty."

Nido waved to his wife and kids as they pulled out on the desert floor. "You said, 'send for me a bride.'"

"I must have been drunk."

Marcos followed and he seemed amused and interested, because it reminded him, he wanted a squaw girl for a wife.

"You drink a little. We only speak our true minds when we are a little—say, a little drunk, si amigo."

Buck returned, "You sure as hell think you are smart."

"You are getting me mixed with those worthless friends at the bar."
Nido didn't mean to be insulting, but he annoyed Buck when he thought he knew what Buck needed out of life, when Buck didn't know what he needed himself.

"You say as plain as day, 'Write for me a pretty little girl—I am tired of waiting for Zulinda to give up her Mexican friends.'"

Buck couldn't deny that he had probably said that, the way he felt of late. Marcos moved up front and the three rode side by side, but Marcos didn't say a word about a squaw. He didn't want to get Buck mad.

"You said, 'I want a woman of my own. No need to tell her how ol' I am.' Thees is what you say." Nido laughed.

Buck wanted to punch him in the mouth, but it was stretched

out so wide he was afraid he might get his hand caught inside. Marcos, who always had a lot of respect for Buck, laughed too. Buck grew mad as a wet hen.

Then Marcos seemed to take the matter more seriously—afraid the matter might break into warfare—warned. "Remember, our bullets are for the Apache." But he couldn't help but needle Buck a little. "He learn a lot of things about Buck from Senor Nido."

Buck no longer called Nido a liar, but was facing up to his responsibilities.

The little settlement of Los Colinas was no longer visible as they came to the top of a hill. A faint smoke appeared in the distance. "That was those damn Indians, settled down along the trail ready to plunder," Buck said, knowing they were cooking a horse.

"I tell you, I only write for people who no write. Why you not write your own letter?"

"Shud up," Buck sounded off. "There are more important things to do than argue."

They dropped over a slight hill and there in the distance was what looked like a wagon. Buck pulled out his scope. Sure enough, it was a wagon loaded with supplies and a wheel missing. Two Indians were looking over the goods. The three urged their horses on, raising a cloud of dust. The Indians took more time than they should have in picking out what they could carry away. Before the riders were within gunshot, the two Apaches each grabbed a bolt of colorful yardage, some pots and pans, and then galloped away. The ends of the yardage unrolled and flapped in the breeze. It was a pretty sight, but grim.

Weighted down with their goods, the riders caught up with the Indians. They turned around, leveled their guns at the riders and fired, but on a fast run it was hard for them to aim while turned backward. Buck brought one down and Marcos the other. Nido could hardly keep his heavy rifle leveled while on a run, so he didn't fire.

They rode on to where they were supposed to meet with John and his vaqueros. Before they got there, they could see in the distance what was a wagon train stopped by the Apaches.

John had holed up in a canyon. The Apaches had settled just to the west of him and his men had dug in behind huge boulders prepared for an attack. John had grown impatient waiting for Buck to return with Nido. "What the hell took you?"

Buck pointed to Nido. "He got me into this mess and he's going to help get me out of it."

"There's nothing wrong with a good wife, Buck," his brother commented.

"I suppose not, but this be my first time. I want to do what is right for her. I don't want to talk about it now," Buck said to John, "You've been here for a while. What do you have planned?"

The men were scattered out, hugging the boulders for protection and eating what they brought from home, which didn't amount to much. "Marques is up the canyon, camped for the summer. He plans to attack every wagon train that passes along the trail. He has a permanent camp which means women and children. They haven't much to eat so they try to take plenty from the wagons. They eat someone's horse every day."

Buck grabbed a tortilla from a food basket and talked while he ate. "I say we move up the canyon gradually, use the boulders for protection. With our long rifles we can pick off a few Indians. Nido needs a rock to rest his piece on when he shoots. This is a good place for him."

"We could make a rush and join the wagon train," John said to Buck.

"No, they're pinned down on the flat and don't have any water," Buck said.

"If you stay here by this tiny stream, the water will give you the advantage for a long battle," John said.

Nido sat quietly in the shade of a small tree, surveying the situation. It had been a long while since he had gone out to help stop the Indians from overrunning the territory. His face was red from the hot sun. Cradling his heavy gun on his lap, he looked worn, but in a few days he'd be his young self again. Marcos was lounging with the vaqueros, trying to catch a few winks. They didn't try to make any reasoning; whatever decisions were made, they would follow.

The Apaches knew a posse was hidden among the rocks, but avoided the vaqueros and rode out to circle the wagon train. Buck could hear the noise in the distance. The Indians were firing too often, wasting their bullets, but it didn't sound good.

The Indians knew they had a better chance with the inexperienced wagon train than they did with the tough vaqueros in the canyon. Buck decided he had to get on the desert floor to even things up a bit. He worked his way up the canyon wall on foot. There were plenty of ledges for protection, and once out on a flat ledge, he brought his scope out and looked through the haze of the simmering heat from the desert earth.

The wagons were in a circle, backed up against the cliff for protection on one side. Some of the wagons were turned over as a barricade and the store goods piled up as a wall. There appeared to be a stagecoach, which caused Buck's heart to give a loud thump.

John ambled up the hill, and then pulled his scope for a minute. Buck valued his opinion. Even though he sometimes irked Buck, Buck knew John was more reliable than he was. Buck considered himself the hireling.

The Indians rode around the wagon train. When they came to the cliff, they were forced to turn around and go in the opposite direction. That was where the wagon train had the advantage. There was a moment's pause and even the poorest shot took a toll among the braves. Buck's crew needed every advantage they could get; they were outnumbered ten to one.

John and Buck decided the wagon train was holding their own. They should rush out there and show the braves how brave they were. They slid down the hill and moved cautiously along the canyon taking pot shots at a few Indians, thereby putting pressure on those below to take the braves away from the wagon train.

Marcos and Buck left their horses behind and slipped among the rocks. They picked off a few Indians and bided their time. They weren't ready to do battle on two fronts. Those in the canyon became excited and sent scouts out to warn the attackers of the wagon train and consequently they gradually began riding back into Indian camp. That was the way they had planned it. And they couldn't have asked for anything better. But Buck knew there had been an abundance of great braves; you couldn't have all luck. There was also an abundance of great boulders that had washed down the canyon over the centuries. It would have been an enjoyable spot for a picnic with the tiny stream winding along, bordered by green willows and towering cottonwood, but they didn't have time to enjoy the shade or the scenery.

Since most of the Indians had now moved back to their permanent camp in the canyon, Buck decided it was time for him to move in with the wagon train. Marcos was anxious to go along. Where there was danger, Buck never had to ask Marcos to come along.

"Two men won't help much," John commented.

"We can give them moral support."

John had his vaqueros and Nido to hold their position. Marcos and Buck rode up the steep grade and looked down on the flat lands. With no shade, the heat was intense. Seeing no Indians, they made a dash for the wagon train. Buck estimated the distance to be a little over a mile. If there were Indians, they were hidden in the clumps of bushes. The distance could be one dangerous mile, but their horses having drunk from the tiny stream were fresh and strong.

Near the wagon train were more boulders, broken loose from the great cliff that overshadowed the tiny camp. They stopped, shouted and held up their firearms, so as not to be mistaken for the Apache, even though they looked nearly as dirty and ragged.

They were finally admitted to the encampment and surrounded by scared settlers. Buck commiserated with the Frenchman. He seemed to be in charge. "Sorry to see you lose your wagon train again, Frenchy." Buck hadn't met the man before, but he had heard so much about him that they felt that everyone knew him.

"I have to lose it yet, mon ami."

"His name was Alexander Du Lac. He was handsome and a little stout. He hadn't shaved since he left St. Joe, Missouri, weeks back. His hair was black, almost as black as that of the Mexicans and Apaches. He was a fine figure, a determined young man. Buck stood back, wondering how he could save these settlers who didn't know they had driven into hell.

The Frenchman's trousers hung low with the weight of his sidearms; having been robbed the year before, he was prepared to save his goods and those of the settlers this trip. Buck didn't know which was the more important. He spoke with an accent, and offered each of the newcomers a tin cup of wine. He had one wagon loaded with fifty gallon barrels. In the heat, the sweet purple juice was oozing out around bungholes. It would be a shame to see the wine spoil, but the lot that hung around Zulinda's cantina would drink anything.

There were about thirty wagons in the outfit. Twelve belonged to the Frenchman. He sold goods here about in the territory. The rest of the wagons belonged to settlers, mostly people in their thirties heading west. They were a sturdy lot, ambitious, but knew very little about fighting Apaches. Buck felt sorry as hell for each one of them. There were about twelve dutiful wives, looking worn beyond their years. They followed where their husbands led them. If they weren't pleased with the way things went, they kept their opinion to themselves the best way they could. There were a half dozen children of various ages running around, and like their elders, they didn't know what they were getting into.

Buck was not sure all the men were interested in farming;

there were only four plows to 18 wagons, but Frenchy had a half load of plows. He would sell them to the Mexicans.

After the men finished their wine, they tried to find the place where they could get the best of the Indians.

"We don't have time for small talk," Marcos told Buck.

Buck said, "We have to help these poor devils get ready for another attack by the Apache." It wasn't Marcos' nature to talk much or take charge, but they needed someone to show them how to stand up against an attack.

Several men in store clothes got out of the stagecoach and stood around with the Frenchman's new rifles in hand. They scarcely knew how to use them and none of them had ever killed an Indian. That was a disadvantage they would have to overcome in a hurry if they wanted to be of any help in saving themselves.

Buck tried to disperse the crowd. He told them they needed to throw a hill of dirt up in front of the wagons. "The Apaches have rifles as well as bows. They have to get closer to shoot with bows; that's when you shoot them down. A rifle will go through a wagon bed, it's no real protection. You all have shovels, use them. Dig from the inside; throw the dirt up against the wagon. That might save a few lives and that will give you a cool place to lie in, since the sun is out, hot."

Buck didn't have time to waste his breath. "You have to learn fast." He was interested in the stagecoach. Was the girl in it or not? The women went about their business of cooking as Buck asked them, but the men followed him around. Buck became their new found leader. And they didn't mean to leave him. Frenchy's scout was to lead them to California, but no one had seen him for days.

Buck turned Prince loose to nibble on a few sprouts of grass, but he wanted something better, and nudged Buck from time to time, hoping he would come up with something, like a half gallon of oats. Prince didn't like the grass that everyone had stepped on and followed Buck until he came to the stagecoach, where he gave Buck and extra hard shove with his nose. When Buck regained his balance, he tied Prince to the back end of the coach.

The driver of the stage was a man of forty. He looked worn, sitting on the driver's seat hanging onto his long rifle as if he had made the trip before. There was a man with experience, and Buck thought he had some sense until he scanned the area and when he saw no Indians, he said, "I think we could make a break for it."

The sun was hanging low in the west and smoke from the Indian fires was drifting in the wagon train's direction.

"You wait till morning," Buck called up to the driver. "They would ambush you at night." Buck didn't tell him that he expected things to be worse in the morning.

Then Buck told him in general, since most were still hanging around. "For those of you who have not fought the Apache, have probably already found out, when they give their battle cry, it chills the blood in your vein. The best way to offset that is to give your own cry, a good Texas yell.

Then the coach driver pointed in the distance where smoke was rising directly from the floor of the canyon. The wind was dying down and the smoke curled upward blanking out the setting sun.

"They are trying to burn us out," the stagecoach driver shouted as he pointed toward the canyon.

Buck said, "They caught one of the Frenchman's horses and are planning to roast it. With their bellies full, they'll keep us pinned down for a long while."

Several men were throwing up embankment in the front of their wagons. On the sheltered side, their wives were cooking. The Frenchman was walking around with new shovels for those who needed them. He was a generous cuss, but Marques Colorado might still get them in the long run.

The Frenchman heard what the stagecoach driver said, "They not burn us out, they need the grass for their horses, they only want my supply of beans and flour."

The driver climbed down from his seat and joined Buck and the Frenchman, who still had shovels in his hands.

"Do you think we've been driven off our trail?" the stagecoach driver asked Buck.

"You're getting close to the Garett spread, if that means anything," Buck answered.

A very timid-looking blond girl opened the coach door wide enough to speak to the driver. "Did I hear someone say that the Garett ranch was near?"

If that was Suzy Carver, she was more beautiful than Buck had imagined. Frightened, her eyes were round and a sparkling blue, but a little red from dust smoke and lack of sleep. Buck went into shock and failed to identify himself. She would be just right for Jewell. Nido would say Buck was a fool, the younger the better. But Buck thought it would be a crime to impose himself onto such a beautiful young girl. Sure Buck liked her, but he always wanted to be fair to the other person. If she had been the old biddy Buck had suggested to Elena, she would have been just right for Buck.

An unsuspected shot rang out. The girl pulled her hand in and closed the door. Frenchy, who had been talking alternately to the driver and Buck, was also struck by the beauty of the girl. He said to the driver, "Your passenger—she ees very pretty—what is her name?"

"Suzy Carver, a nurse from Chicago."

Buck's heart jumped, but not with joy.

The stagecoach driver had no fear for himself; he checked his rifle. "Don't get any ideas," he told the Frenchman. "She's betrothed to some son-of-a bitch by the name of Garett, trying to hang onto a ranch out here in hell. He doesn't deserve her, bringing a bride out to this God forsaken country."

Buck looked at the driver. His face was thin and drawn; he was interested in delivering all his passengers safely. He started to climb up on the stage for a better view. Buck didn't like what he said about the Garetts. Buck could have slugged him, knocked out a few of those tobacco stained teeth, but he was right. At Buck's suggestion, he climbed back down and took his place under the stage, behind a pile of dirt. Things were moving fast. Buck had to lie down beside the driver. After the driver's uncalled for remarks about the Garetts, Buck had no intention of identifying himself. Buck promised himself that he would save the girl for Jewell.

Prince whinnied. Buck knew what that meant. He raised up and brought down a half-naked wild man who had sneaked in from behind one of the boulders. Buck had to reload.

The Frenchman wanted a second look at the girl. He opened the door to the stagecoach; the girl was curled up in a corner terrified from the noise of firing and the noise of the shooting Indians. He couldn't see much, but extended his hand encouragingly. "Please Miss Suzy; there are far safer places than the stagecoach. She stared down at the Frenchman, wild eyed and shaky. For the Frenchman, Buck was sure it was love at first sight.

Buck knocked another Indian rolling. The men from the wagon train were taking their toll. It was too much for the braves; they started to retreat as fast as they had appeared. It was getting dark and Buck supposed they would retire for the night, eat a chunk of that horse, remember their dead, then go to sleep, determined to wipe out the wagon train the next day.

The Frenchman was determined, and Buck nearly choked with regret, such a tender young girl exposed to the dangers of the west. If Buck couldn't save her for Jewell, the Frenchman and the girl should have a running chance.

"Miss Suzy. Please come out. Zee Apache retire for the night." He took her hand and drew her toward himself.

In the dark, Suzy's eyes were round with fright. Buck was scared for her. The war with the Apache hadn't really started yet, and Buck knew he should be protecting Suzy.

The Frenchman helped the girl from the coach. Her white uniform was wrinkled from sitting on it, and covered with dust. He had hold of her pretty white hand and didn't turn loose while he introduced himself. Buck couldn't help but think, is this what Suzy Carver asked for when she accepted his proposal. The stagecoach driver called out, "Indians." Buck dashed around and to the other side of the coach and knocked over an Indian scout lurking behind a boulder in the semi darkness. That was when Buck decided he had to have a guard or two in the rocks so the Indians couldn't sneak up on the wagon train during the night.

Buck's gun made a right smart crack when it went off, and Suzy threw herself against the Frenchman for protection. He held her sympathetically with one arm while he reached into his hip pocket for a flask. The coach driver brought out a tin cup and held it while Frenchy filled it. The driver took the flask while Frenchy offered the cup to the girl. "Drink this Miss Suzy—wine ees good for the nerves."

If Suzy was supposed to be a nurse, she began to feel ashamed of herself the way she was acting. Buck thought she should be taking care of the wounded, but he supposed in her initial shock with the west her fear of the Indians came first.

"I'm acting like a baby," were her first words and they sounded music to Buck, a beautiful feminine voice. He was more determined than ever to turn her over to Jewell. She would make a great boon to the ranch, to the west.

The Frenchman tried to assure her, "You act very normal." He loved his chance to comfort her. Suzy smiled for the first time, and to Buck's annoyance, it would be at the Frenchman. She took the cup offered to her. Hoping to alleviate her fright, she gulped down the entire contents and grabbed her throat. She stood there straight as a barrel cactus and shuddered. Buck admired her. She looked different from the others, nice, just in the right places. Buck could have admired the girl more, but he had one eye out for more sneaky Indians who didn't have sense enough to go back to their camp and have a great slice of that roasted horse. Buck didn't eat horse, but it did smell good from a distance, more than a mile away.

Sometimes the Frenchman wished he had never outfitted his first supply wagon, but had settled down permanently on his land to tend the corn and hoe his grapes. There was a certain amount of adventure stored in him or he never would have lasted in the supply business.

But Frenchy was restless, which bordered onto romantic. His older brother had outfitted a supply train and sold his goods somewhere in the southwest and continued on to California, never to be heard of again. Frenchy's younger brother Xavier landed in New Orleans during an outbreak of yellow fever. After his friends who came with him died of the disease, he went north to a French settlement in St. Joe, Missouri and by accident he found his brother Alexander living in northwestern Kansas. Xavier bought a farm just across the road from his brother.

None of the Du Lac boys had been sedentary Completely against their father's wishes, they had left the southern part of France, La Bastide, to become a part of the Louisiana purchase, a Frenchman's dream. The French didn't have to change their language, the reason why the French spoke with a thick dialect. Wanderlust ran deep within Frenchy's veins. Money was not the object. In every little village, Xavier had always enquired of his eldest brother.

All of a sudden an Indian came riding in. In the dark, Buck swung his rifle around and tumbled him to the ground.

Meanwhile, Suzy who had scarcely been out of the coach since it joined up with the wagon train that afternoon, stumbled around acting a little wobbly. Buck began to believe that the trip had affected her. She placed her hand against the coach for support. Then to the Frenchman, still hanging around to admire her she said, "There must be some wounded to take care of." She reached in the coach for her bag and Frenchy led her past several cooking fires to an overturned wagon where three men lay back in the dust exhausted, trying to ignore their situation. For a fourth it was already too late.

Frenchy introduced Suzy to the most severely wounded.

"Dave my mule skinner." He was a big, heavy set man of fifty, his beard partially graying. His right leg was useless. He had his trousers ripped aside where a broken piece of bone was sticking out of the fleshy part of his leg.

Suzy looked around at the flickering campfire that lit up the night. "I'll need a lantern," she said to Frenchy. He set out immediately. Suzy, disregarding her white uniform, kneeled down beside the mule skinner. "I'm a nurse," she said before examing the wound. Few people had ever heard of a nurse. There were scarcely any in the east, but none in the west.

"The lucky cuss," Buck said to himself as he looked out at the dark night, hoping the last of the Apaches were eating by now.

4

"I have been trained to assist a doctor and a lot more."

The mule skinner was sitting in the sand, still hot from the afternoon sun. When he fully understood what the duties of a nurse were supposed to be, he leaned back and relaxed. Suzy put her hand on the man's hairy leg. It was crusty with blood and no one had tried to wash it.

When Frenchy came back with the lantern, he leveled off a spot in the sand and set the lantern there, where the light would shine on Dave's wounded leg.

"Dave is the only one who needs the wine," Suzy said. "Not me, I feel a little drunk already."

By that time Frenchy learned what a nurse did. Her every thought was his command. The Frenchman was also a cooper. He made the barrels on his farm for the wine from his vineyard. He made the wine in his oversized cellar and at that time he unloaded the wine wagon, and the safest place from flying arrows was behind his barrels.

"We have plenty of wine," Frenchy said, almost bowing to the girl as he hurried away for more wine for Dave.

"And some water to wash his leg," she called after the gracious Frenchman.

Frenchy took a granite pot from a wagon and pulled a plug from one of the bullet holes. He caught the wine as it poured out from the pressure built up by the sun. When the flow slowed, he pounded the plug back into the barrel, took the pot back and set it next to the wounded man. Then he hurried after water. Nearly everyone had a barrel for water; the water in the pond was mud.

Suzy washed the dry blood from the wounded man's leg and covered the area with a white gauze. She still looked a little wobbly from the one cup of wine and perspired heavily, but this was perhaps from the number of people standing around watching her.

Buck got up from where he was watching Suzy, and mingled with the crowd. "Go back to your supper," he said quietly to several people until the numbers started thinning.

As Suzy became better adjusted to the poor light, she sorted out her instruments and placed them on a satchel while the mule skinner drank several cups of wine. Buck watched the girl with awe. It was as though an angel of mercy had descended from heaven to administer to the wounded. Frenchy dipped his cup into the pot and handed it to the mule skinner; that was his fifth cup.

"Please lie down flat, Dave," Suzy commanded.

Dave obeyed and closed his eyes; Suzy was glad not to have him starting at her.

The bone was broken and had to be set in place then bandaged. She pulled on the foot, but the bone did not set in place, and it hurt terribly.

She wiped the excess blood aside. The mule skinner squirmed with pain.

"Hold his legs," she said to the Frenchman. He complied gladly. "This is going to hurt when I pull on your foot to reconnect the break." By that time Dave was nearly drunk. But a man had to be plenty drunk not to feel the pain. Buck was watching; he could only compare Suzy with the lily that bloomed in the hot dry desert. But a lily never lasted long in the hot sun. "Let it hurt," Dave gritted his teeth, prepared for the pain, as Suzy pulled on the foot and shoved the broken bone together.

A number of men who should have found something better to do were again standing around. Buck didn't have the gall to suggest that they turn in for the night. They probably wouldn't have slept; they were too unnerved from the happenings of the day. They would sleep, when around Apache, only when they became dog-tired.

With a gauze Suzy stemmed the flow of blood. The wound was worse than any rifle shot, but Dave was lucky. The mule skinner was a strong man and the ordeal took a lot out of him. "If you like, drink another cup of wine," Suzy said and shook her head to remove a long hair from her eyes. Then she looked through her collection of needles encased in a heavy paper folder, "I have to sew up the wound. The jagged bone cut your skin. You would have been a cripple the rest of your life if we hadn't set the bone properly," she said to Dave, who was lying on a pillow feeling numb. Frenchy handed Suzy a cup. "Mostly water," he said. "Easier for you to drink." By that time it was totally dark except for the fires burning around several wagons as people finished washing their dishes. There was no need to conceal the camp; the Indians knew where they were. They would be back full force, come morning, to wipe out the wagon train.

The horses in their enclosure were as restless as the people; they whinnied from thirst and had to be tied up to keep them from breaking loose and burying themselves in the mud in the nearby stream that had almost dried up.

By the flickering light of the lantern, Suzy sewed up Dave's torn flesh and bandaged it tightly with white sheeting ripped from a bolt of Frenchy's material. Then Frenchy brought three straight twigs from his wood pile. In no time the girl had the splints fastened around the wounded leg so the skinner couldn't move it in his sleep and undo the set. "When the wine wears off you'll probably not sleep. It will hurt for several days," she said looking at Dave. He was in a stupor from the wine and didn't answer. "Try and not move your leg for several days."

Suzy had a strip of blanket wrapped around Dave's leg so the rough splints wouldn't rub his leg raw. "In the morning, I'll wrap the splints, and put a new bandage on your leg.

Then Suzy turned to the lesser wounded, ate very little for supper and lay back down behind the embankment, curled up next to her patients. The Frenchman was nearby. Buck would have been glad to stand guard on the other side, but he had work to do.

At the bottom of the cliff, was the played out stream that ran by the camp. In the spring, after a snowy winter, there was generally water. Over the years, a small lake formed, but this year it was at most a pond of mud, a remnant of the year's light rainfall. That was where some of the horses had already waded, deeper and deeper, in desperation for the last drop of water. Some were stuck in the mud and still struggling; by morning they would be dead. Buck rounded up the owners of the horses, assuring them that the Indians had retired for the night. "If you want to save your horses, I'll help you pull them out of the mud."

Four men came to help. They took two ropes and threw them over the neck of the first horse and fastened the ropes around the saddle horn of two different mounts on firm ground with a steady pull they soon had one horse on its feet and it was able to walk out of the mud with the assist. The men stood their distance as the horse shook to free itself of excess mud. When they had all the animals out, they pulled some of the long grass along the edge of the pond for the animals to eat. It was the only greenery in the area and they also fed it to the animals in the enclosure.

Without water since morning, the animals were anxious for anything moist, even though it was tough grass. The horses whinnied as the men approached with a small bucket of grass for each horse and a big bucket full for a milk cow tied behind a settler's wagon. It was the wee hours of the morning before Buck turned in for a few winks of sleep. There were men still walking around with their rifles while their wives lay awake wide eyed with fear. Buck was awakened early by the stagecoach driver singing the blues to the Frenchman. The coach had been due in Tucson three or four days ago. Frenchy was little concerned. "Bad to be behind schedule." But he might not get back to Kansas early enough to make new wine, if it took too long to sell his goods.

The Frenchman had a lot of special rifles. He had to keep them from the Indians. If they got their hands on the latest weapons, it wouldn't be safe for anyone in the territory.

When the sun came up, Buck knew he could sleep no longer even though he only had a few hours sleep. He got up and ventured his opinion in fighting Marques Colorado. So many people thought, when they hadn't seen Indians for a few hours, that they can amble down the trail as usual. But the Indians were out for plunder, and it would take any number of the wagon train men and the mule skinners to stop that.

Buck ventured, "You want to get out of this alive, you won't get more than a mile down the trail and you'll get your ticket punched, for sure."

Buck produced his scope and he and a man climbed up the side of the cliff where they could look down on the vicinity of wickiups and grass shelters.

The coach-driver puffed nervously on a cheroot. "I have a man, J.J. Walters, offered me five hundred dollars if I could get him to California in a month," he said to Frenchy.

Frenchy too, was concerned. When could he move on? He took Buck's eyepiece first, lifted it and looked westward for only a few seconds, then handed the instrument to the coach driver. "I think this J.J. fellow keep his money."

The Apache were dancing nearly naked around a huge fire. That seemed silly to Buck; it was going to be hot enough later during the day. They had gorged themselves on horse meat the night before. Now, with a little burnt meat for breakfast they would be able to fight all day. Buck let the driver know the facts, and he was blunt. He understood better that way.

The driver was beginning to understand the situation they were in. "There are several hundred out there working themselves up for an attack." That's the way it was.

Buck said, "I estimate that there are ten to our one, all sturdy braves."

Bob was a quick witted young man who loved to roam the hills and face danger. "Next year I may not have a job."

"Your whole family will be glad, your sister above all," Frenchy said, showing that he knew Bob's family.

Suzy got up looking somewhat refreshed. She moved about to see that the wounded were comfortable. They were awake except the mule skinner, who was still sleeping off the effects of the wine.

Frenchy immediately became aware that Suzy was moving about. It was like having a doctor with the wagon train. Buck knew that Frenchy envied every man Suzy touched. "When one settle down he need a woman like that."

If Buck had been a younger man, he would have made himself known and crowded the Frenchman out of the picture. He still kept thinking, Suzy would make an ideal wife for Jewell.

"I understand she is promised to some rancher." Frenchy wished he knew more about the man.

"Garett," Buck supplied the name. He had not used the name when he introduced himself and probably never would. He was only standing by for Suzy's protection. "His brother owns the Garett spread, goes on for miles."

Buck got out his scope to study the Indians lined up along the rim of the canyon. "He could hear John and his men taking potshots at those who remained below. The Indians were bewildered; they didn't seem to know whether to wade in and take the stragglers hidden behind boulders or to go after the wagon train. They were bent on taking supplies, rifles. That would make them a powerful force. Their immediate plans seemed to have been affected by the loss of their braves so early in the morning.

Everyone went to his position, waiting for the attack; most of the women belted a sidearm around their waist. Frenchy was standing in back of his barrels. His vaqueros were out in the front line of defense. His skinners were standing at attention like the minute men in their brown earth jackets. Most of them had been through this the summer before and the wagons lost. Even David with the broken ankle stood at attention, favoring his leg until Suzy voiced her concern, "You better lie down; any movement will delay healing. Dave and Frenchy were still talking to the scout and to Buck. "I theenk I no like thees Garett fellow," he said pensively as he watched Suzy check Dave's leg. She then sat beside him in the depression dug for protection of the wounded. Suzy didn't look as frightened as she had the evening before; she was a real boon to the wagon train.

By that time everyone was behind an overturned wagon leaning into the dirt they had dug up. They all felt better protected and prepared to fight.

But Frenchy was still trying to talk Bob out of going for help while the Indians were occupied, preparing for an attack.

By that time, Frenchy knew the same as Buck knew, that one man on the desert floor alone was a lost cause.

The Frenchman knew his family, which led him to say, "Your sister die if I let you get killed."

A heavy well dressed man Buck had never met before walked over. He had a gold chain over his huge expanse of chest. "My name is Walters, J.J. Walters. I am offering anyone five hundred dollars who can get me out of here and to California in a month. He seemed to be talking directly to Buck. Buck seemed to know that he had made the same offer to the stagecoach driver.

"Money won't get you out of this delay in a week," Buck said to make it sound better. He knew a lot of them would never make it to California. "In a week all the horses will be dead from lack of water. Get yourself a rifle instead of those sidearms, and get behind those barrels. Learn to defend yourself."

Bob was chewing on the last of Frenchy's jerked meat. His mouth was full and he could hardly talk. He pointed to his jaw that bulged. "The longer I chew it the bigger it gets. That was the way with jerky, but it had a lot of strength in it." Then he spoke to the Frenchman as they were all hanging around the barrels waiting for the Indians to show. "Frenchy, get me a fresh horse and I'll ride for help," Bob said.

Buck was beginning to get mad at the stupid bastard. "There are no fresh horses—they all need water. The Indians have all the fresh horses, they'll run you down."

Finally Buck put his foot down rather than allow the young man to get killed in broad daylight. "Wait until tonight—maybe you'll get a mile or so down the trail. If I think it best, maybe I'll go with you." That made the Frenchman feel better; he didn't seem to worry about Buck getting killed.

Du Lac was a generous, good-natured young man; he had agreed to accompany the wagon train to Arizona territory and no farther. There were no charges for his services. But Bob had promised to take charge of the wagon train for the rest of the route to California. He seemed to be an irresponsible young man, always on the go, bringing in game for food, if there was game to be had. If they got out of this alive, Buck felt sorry for those who might follow Bob to California.

Buck was getting restless and got out his trusted telescope to check the Apaches again, wondering why they hadn't attacked. He climbed part way up the cliff so he could look down on the Indian camp. Marques Colorado wanted the wagon train to know that he was still there and would be there until he got supplies. Buck adjusted the lens on the scope. The solemn bastard stood there on the crest of the hill, looking his way. There was no doubt that he was in charge. His braves loved him because of his new aggressiveness. He was chewing on a huge horse bone and Buck could almost hear his booming voice. Mito his young protégé, skinny as a rail, looked the same as his brother, the same as the day Buck bargained with him for the return of Elena. Buck could tell by the dress that the kid had been initiated into a brave. He stood there solemnly watching Marques Colorado, his great hero. He hoped to be a great hero someday, mean as his dad.

Buck could almost hear his elder saying, "Why you not eat?" Mito looked as if he worried more about the upcoming battle than the chief himself.

The kid's brother, according to Buck's way of thinking, was the one who had made the deal for Elena so expensive. He was learning to bargain, or Buck might have had some store goods to put down on the ranch. It wouldn't have taken much. Buck never spent all his money for drinks in those days; that came later. "Eat," Marques said. Buck could almost hear the chief shouting at the youngster. "The fight is not over yet—brave must eat."

It was unusual for one so young to be concerned about a battle, but Buck supposed concern so young was what would make him a great chief. The kid pointed in Buck's direction. He was concerned with all the wagons. The eastern sun reflected from the Indians' rifles as they held them high, ready to ride into battle. Buck said, "We have wagons and we will keep them if I have anything to say about it."

Still, they hesitated. They probably needed shells for their guns. If they had bullets they would never quit fighting. That was the reason why they hadn't attacked this morning. But they would get bullets, the chief would assure the young man, even if he didn't know how to get them himself. If he didn't get bullet, the kid wouldn't look up to him. The great chief needed to be idolized.

Maybe they weren't going to attack; just let their horses die of thirst. The kid and the chief were on the outs. Buck could have laughed at them under different circumstances. Marques seemed almost thunder struck by the kid's audacity. Buck adjusted the lens on his scope, this was getting good. The chief kicked the kid in the rear. The kid better learn to shut his mouth if he wants to grow up

The Apaches are not one to fight at night, but Buck knew something had to be amiss or they would make better use of the day. They were without water for the horses, oh they were getting a trickle, and the Indians were without bullets, but they had plenty of arrows and could shoot them almost as fast as Buck could shoot his rifle. Arrows made a more jagged wound and were sometimes smeared with venom. Buck folded the telescope and walked down the cliff. Small loose rocks followed him down the hill.

Buck advised the camp, "If you want to bake bread, now is the time; the Indians have a hang up." Buck figured John was picking off a few; that may have been the reason they hadn't attacked the wagon train all morning.

Nearly everyone had curled up in their blankets early that evening, hoping for a good night's sleep. There was plenty of new bread in the camp, but Buck was walking around camp eating Frenchy's old dry sour-dough. The moon came out and the stars shined down on them. Buck wrapped a blanket around his shoulders and walked to the guards next to their rocks. Buck never slept much when danger was at hand. He guessed it was nearly midnight by the progress of the moon. The guards walked back and forth between two huge boulders. They looked regularly in the direction of the Indian encampment. Buck looked up from time to time, and raised up to pull the blanket more securely around his frame. Then Buck saw a shadow move along the ground.

When the guards turned to peer in that direction the shadow lay still. When the guards turned to look a different direction the shadow moved forward, like a cat sneaking up on a bird. When the guards turned back the shadow lay as still as the rocks around it. Finally the shadow moved past the guards and was nearing the wagon train. By that time, Buck had his gun at ready and followed the shadow. It was that dumb kid. He was worth more to the camp in a deal than dead. Besides, Buck didn't want to kill a kid, even if he was an Indian. He moved around until he found some shells, neatly stacked in crates behind one of the overturned wagons. He took a heavy carton and was crawling out of camp. He rested and opened the box and put some of the shells in his knee high moccasins.

The closest guard was sitting on the rock nodding, and then he filled his pipe and lit it to keep awake. The shadow crawled cautiously, inching along. Buck was following him. When it was determined he was tired, Buck pounced on him, slapping his hand over his mouth lest they both get their tickets punched. Buck tied a rope around his hands in back, another rope to his ankles, and then he stood up and shouted to the guard. "Hey Vaquero, it's me. Don't shoot, it's me. I have a prisoner." When the kid tried to run, Buck yanked the rope and he went down.

"Help me get a horse," Buck said to the guard. "I'm going to ride into the Apache camp and bargain."

The guards jumped from their rocks and came forward. The moon was under a cloud, but it was early morning.

They took a horse from the enclosure, and set Mito in the saddle. Buck held the rope in case he wanted to bolt. When they got to the rim of the canyon the sun was up.

Marques Colorado had missed the kid and gone up the hill looking for him. He was followed by two of the most trusted braves. Buck was glad to be away from their camp. With luck he could handle five by himself. He still had the kid on the horse in front of him. Buck rode in bravely, knowing they would hold their fire. Marques Colorado loved the kid, even if he wouldn't admit it. Being on a lower level than Buck had irked the chief. He had not always been that way. A little kindness from civilization must have brushed off on him at one time. But Buck knew he was a mean bastard; he hadn't always been that way. He had held his son-in-law, Cochise, back for a time.

Cochise had once gone to a small restaurant for food. The cook threw the dishwater out the back door just as Cochise tried to enter. Cochise had been aggressive ever since

Buck didn't know who wanted to kill him first, Cochise, or the boy who went for bullets.

"You fool kid, you could have been killed," was his first outburst of affection, but in Apache it sounded like hate.

"But I got bullets," Mito said as he kicked his knee length moccasins and bullets spilled to the ground. Buck had allowed him to take them because they would not fit Indian rifles.

"Bullets ha! Marques chief here. Marques give orders." He pounded his chest and threw it forward. He was wrapped in newly stolen yardage, yellow with black polka dots, not yet made into a shirt. Mito was dressed the same; it made them look distinctive.

Buck had bargained for Elena, but now he had his way, at least for a few minutes. Buck had his protégé and wondered if the chief had any real feelings as he did. Buck knew Elena had gone through hell, forced to live with the Apache braves. He had to bargain fast, before the camp got wind of what was happening or Buck would be like a grasshopper on an ant hill.

Buck had the two braves in front of him covered with his rifle, but another snuck his way around and came up from behind. He jumped on Buck's horse and somehow yanked the boy to the ground. Buck whirled with his rifle and caught the intruder in the side of the head with the barrel of his gun. He dropped to the ground and lay there. With the boy removed, that was the signal for the others to take him, not alive, but spare the horse.

Buck took the one leveling his rifle with a bullet in the chest, the one with the bow with his ready to smoke sidearm.

Mito lay prostrate on the ground, looking up at the great chief as though he were pleading for his very life. He got up cautiously and Marques kicked him in the rear and he sprawled out among the shells. By that time the Indian on the ground had recovered and climbed on the back of Buck's horse. He had Buck by the back of the neck, but Buck clung to his saddle horn. He was choking Buck, but Buck used his free hand to pry him loose. Buck could hear the whole tribe whooping as they came up the hill; but he had no way to guide the horse. He gouged him with his spurs. The horse gave a lurch, and turned away from the shouting and in the direction of the wagon train. Buck had caught his last breath some time ago when he punched the Apache in the stomach with his elbow. He turned loose of Buck's neck, but as he slid around, he grabbed the back of Buck's saddle. Buck slowed the horse and he spread out on his rump.

Buck was in control again. The Indian was doing no harm so he left him hang there. When Buck came to a sizable patch of cactus, he gouged the hands loose from the back of the saddle and dumped him. Buck figured the fighting would be long over before that Indian could join in.

John was closer than the wagon train, so Buck headed in that direction and the protection of the boulders. It was still early in the morning and the fighting hadn't started in earnest yet. Buck saw some of John's men concealed behind rocks. They were down below and he was higher up the canyon. He gave a whoop and they recognized him. When Buck found a likely spot, he nudged his hose down a path to join in with John. Minutes later Buck slid behind rocks; a hail of bullets followed him. Some of the Indians thought he was the only one lost and a dozen came in fast, urging their ponies down the bank. Each vaquero took the closest brave to save shells. After a second of firing, more nearly-naked Indians joined in. In numbers they were not brave, but reckless and as the vaqueros guns belched; they came tumbling down the steep arroyo wall bringing dirt and rocks with them. That was too much for the few Indians still on the rim. They turned tail as fast as they had appeared. Buck's horse found water and drank for a long, long time, and he knew how the other horses with the wagon train felt.

When the firing died down, and everyone had caught their breath, Buck said to John, "I have to get back to the wagon train. The coach and the wagon train are both pinned down." Buck climbed up to the rim of the canyon and figured things out with his scope.

Nido came up in back of Buck and asked, "Is she pretty." Before Buck had a chance to answer he shouted, "You still owe me forty-eight pesos."

5

*B*efore Buck had a chance to leave camp, the Indians came at them in full fury; they were getting smart, some dismounted and scattered behind boulders. Buck shouted at the vaqueros, "Don't let the Indians hide, keep them out in the open," How that was done, Buck didn't know, but he hated to see the Indians use wagon train tactics.

Nido stopped one brave, and then rushed behind the rock where Buck was taking his toll. Apaches rode in at a gallop. "Nido," Buck growled, "this is a hell of a lot of trouble you got me into."

"You don't expect to rescue a fair lady without something going wrong," he shouted to Buck, so he could hear above the noise of the battle. "At one time they used fight fire-spouting dragons to rescue the ladies. We have only to fight a hand full of Indians."

The damn fool annoyed Buck with his education. But this time he didn't say anything back. Buck was beginning to believe he was jealous of

Nido's education. Right now, he had to keep his eye open for sneaky Apaches, but they were easier to spot. Some had abandoned their dirty loincloth and were dolled up in bright colored cloth torn from bolts of yardage.

One bearded old vaquero from the ranch rushed in next to Buck for protection. He was standing there reloading his gun and couldn't help it, but he heard what Nido had to say. He had never learned to read or write and resented any kind of learning, so he said to Nido. "Shad up, We don't have any time for book lernin." To be exact, Sam was a tired old mountain man, but he still had a lot of poop left. He was right. Nido needed to take the battle more seriously. Buck stuck his head out from behind the boulder just in time to stop a brave who had dismounted at a run and was ready to use his gun as a club. Buck dropped the brave like a rock and he lay still.

When the firing stopped a few minutes, a rock and a larger boulder protected Buck from nearby Indians. Buck looked up the canyon with his scope. "They are there. I can see the morning sun reflecting off their Springfields."

Buck knew he couldn't feel right unless he did something. He dashed behind a rock and disposed of another Indian. Buck didn't dare look at him too closely. There wasn't time, but with Sam behind a rock, Buck felt more protected and more determined. He called out, "Keep the Indians pinned down; I want to get back to the wagon train. If only to save the horses. Keep them from digging in the dried up pond. They are getting a little seepage. Someone should urge the men to dig in the right place."

John called to Buck, "You can't go! There are still Indians behind those rocks, waiting for anyone to make a dumb move."

"You all watch—I'm going to ride out of here—if one jumps out, take him before he takes me." John was out of sight. Buck had to shout to make him hear.

"You are a damn fool, Buck." Since John was only Buck's half-brother, sometimes Buck didn't think he cared. But when the chips were down, Buck knew better. Buck walked away from the fighting to the dried up steam where his horse was munching on tall grass. Buck climbed on, and like a fool he started on a gallop up the path that led to the rim of the canyon. Bravery was what the Apache respected most and Buck astonished them so they didn't fire for a minute or two. Buck didn't believe there were more than two or three of them left in the canyon close to the wagon train. Was Buck ever wrong. He was heading for a bank of dirt that might shelter him, when a bullet whizzed by. Someone got the brave, but a second jumped from behind a rock and fired at Buck. The men below couldn't see him; Buck slowed down to tumble him with a shot in the buttock as he dived for protection. Buck looked back, and ducked an almost spent arrow over his head. Buck wasn't used to fighting Indians who hid behind rocks. They showed their bravery by fighting out in the flat. Buck looked back for one last time, and then headed between two boulders to rest the horse when a dirty looking brave jumped astride his mount. He had Buck down fair and square, but no gun. Buck was planning his next move when the brave pulled a long rusty knife from his knee-high moccasin. He was a beefy brave, had always eaten well and sat heavy on Buck's stomach. Buck had wrestled right smart with his friends when he was young. Many a time Buck had been sat on by a bigger fellow. Then his friend would tickle him just for sport, and he could get right up. So the Indian tried to tickle Buck just for amusement, but with his dirty knife. He pulled Buck's shirt up and ran the knife up his ribs and laughed. Buck laughed too. This fellow left a streak of blood where he ran the knife; that is where he made his mistake. He intended to run the knife between Buck's ribs and that would be the end. Anytime Buck was tickled when down, he just automatically got up suddenly. To this day Buck can't absolutely stand being tickled, no matter how big the person. Buck was up and rolled the brave. The knife went a little farther in the dirt than he did.

Buck didn't take time to find out how bad off the Indian was, a posse of his blood brothers were coming up the hill whooping it up. They were out of range for John's men, but fortunately they only had bows. Buck headed for the wagon train as fast as his horse could run and that was purdy fast, since Prince had a good drink of water and felt refreshed.

About a mile later, Buck waved his hat in the air to let the people in the wagon train know who he was. He shouted, "coming in."

Several men gathered around Buck, but he let them know, "We don't have time for idle talk. A dozen or more Apaches are following me—will be here in a minute. Man your posts. They only have bows. Let them get close."

Frenchy came over where Buck was standing; he felt worn from an almost all night tangle with the Apaches. Frenchy handed Buck a cup of wine. "I think you be dead." He sounded concerned.

"There's plenty of time for that," Buck said, trying not to think of the worst. "I need this cup of wine." It was food just like Frenchy claimed. Buck was so worked up that he didn't even feel the effects.

Every time there are no Indians around, Buck had some mule skinners digging in the pond. "If we get a little water, we can save the horses."

Frenchy said, "I think the men give up." He didn't sound as concerned as Buck felt.

"We can't give up." Beyond the enclosure of wagons, a horse came briskly running toward the encampment. The two guards got down to determine whether the animal meant good news or bad. Bob the scout was lying across the saddle, his head hanging low. "It's Bob," one guard called out.

They opened a place in the enclosure and guards led the horse in just ahead of a posse of Indians. Since Buck was up and around most of the night, he didn't know the scout had left without Frenchy's permission. Bob had been scalped. Buck didn't know he had escaped death.

Buck found out the damn fool had refused to give up an elk

he had thrown cross his saddle. Walters was standing near the front of the stagecoach. He had his rifle in hand, looking at the wounded man instead of the incoming Indians. As the guards took Bob from his horse, Walters commented, "I knew he couldn't make it." It was the surly way he said it; Buck didn't know he could say anything nice.

Frenchy was there and helped move the scout over to where Suzy had established her sick ward. To make things more comfortable, he had nailed a canvas to the overturned wagon so the sick rested comfortably in the shade, but all had their guns laid out on their blankets, ready to fill in when trouble broke out.

The new group of Indians stayed at a safe distance with their bows. Buck was glad to know they were short of bullets. But they hung around to make the camp nervous, especially the women. When the women were restless it wore off on the men. Suzy spread out a blanket in the shade for her newest patient. The mule skinner with the leg wound started to get up to make more room, but Suzy said, "Lie still, stretch out your leg." She tried to ascertain the extent of the damage on Bob as Frenchy made him comfortable. "Put him on his stomach," she directed.

Instead of watching the Indians, Walters crowded in, "There's nothing you can do for him but make him more comfortable."

"We can do more than that; I'm going to sew him up." Suzy was kneeling in the dirt beside Bob and smiled up at Frenchy and he was at her command. "Get him some wine."

While waiting for the Indians to come in closer, some of the men were acting too brave for the good of the camp. One stout looking brave, with the most powerful bow, pulled it back and let fly an arrow; it hit one of the overturned wagons with a thud. It only annoyed everyone, but that was getting too close. Buck steadied his rifle on one of the wagons and took the stout fellow in the chest. Another brave, with a sweat band of red around his head turned and pulled further away.

Men were milling around. "Get back to your posts," Buck kept telling them in a kindly way, but none had ever seen a scalped man before. They weren't really afraid of the bows. Several stooped down, looking at the scout as Suzy washed around where she was going to fasten the scalp back.

"Get back to where it's safer. An arrow can be just as deadly as bullets," Buck told the onlookers.

"And more painful," Suzy spoke up for Buck. She was catching on fast. Frenchy had a hip flask and handed it to Bob, who nearly emptied the container before he lay back. Frenchy took the container when he quit drinking and stood there waiting for him to have more. The whole front of his scalp hung loose, the reason he rode in face down on the saddle. "They almost got me, Frenchy." Bob still tried to smile, but he was in pain, great pain, the wine helped. He moaned audibly.

"Drink plenty; I'm going to sew you up." Suzy was leaning against, Bob, washing the clotted blood from his hair. "I have to shave you the best I can, to keep the hair out of the wound." She was too pretty to be all business, but she was all business.

Walters was there, mumbling under his breath. He was always bellyaching because he couldn't get to California fast enough. Buck felt like none of them would ever get to California. "A damn scout that can't find his way at night. There's only one trail and he ran right into the Indians."

Walters walked away scowling at Buck. Buck knew he didn't have any authority to deal with him, but he could bluff. Walters didn't entirely shut up; no one could make him do that. "It's no good to be cited for bravery when you get scalped." Buck agreed with him, but like Buck said, "the man couldn't help himself." Suzy pressed on the scalp occasionally, hoping that the juices exuded would soak into the dry scalp.

Right then, while the Indians were in absence, Buck watched and admired Suzy's nimble fingers as she executed one stitch at a time. But that was no sure sign his scalp would be saved or that Bob would be saved.

Buck was tired of waiting for the Indians to come in close enough for a sure shot; he knew his rifle would only scare them. Frenchy and Buck stood looking at the enemy sitting there on their ponies, waiting them out, like a buzzard waiting for a down and out cow to quit kicking.

"Let me see one of your new rifles, Frenchy." He walked over to one of the overturned wagons and Buck followed. Frenchy took a long barreled rifle from one of the crates, unwrapped it and handed it to Buck. It was covered with thick grease. Buck sighted through the barrel that was lined with the same type of oil to keep it from rusting. Buck found a rag and wiped the barrel clean. Frenchy handed Buck a ramrod with a small piece of cloth. Buck dipped the cloth in a kerosene solution and ran it through the barrel several times. He looked through the barrel and it glittered with the sun. It was a beautiful thunder stick. And he loaded it with one of those special shells that wouldn't fit the Indian guns, and then steadied it on an overturned wagon. He brought a well-decorated Indian within sight. Buck hadn't eaten in 24 hours and his hands shook as if he were an old man. Trying to allow for his shaking hands and the wind flapping the canvas covering, Buck slowly pulled the trigger. The brave dropped and his horse followed the one in front of him. When another Apache came within Buck's sight, he dropped him the same way.

Buck was the only one trying to fire. The rest of the men, not sure of themselves or their rifles, were waiting for the Indians to come within range. There had been around twelve and now there were eight. Buck was leveling his gun again when the Indians gave a whoop and made a bee line in the direction of their camp.

"Very good shot," Frenchy complimented Buck and walked over to keep his wine barrels company. When Buck got there, he was chewing on a huge chunk of bread and sipping wine for breakfast.

Buck put the rifle back in its case. "That be a good weapon you got there; we can't let the Indians get hold of any."

"I have fifty."

"Can I have a cup of that wine and a chunk of bread for breakfast?"

"Thees not wine—thees is food. You not have to ask." With both hands he motioned toward the barrel.

"Then I'll have some food. I feel so shaky; I don't know how I hit those bastards."

Buck sat down to enjoy the bread. It had a sour taste and the wine was sweet and nourishing. Buck sagged down and leaned against the soft canvas of the overturned wagon and tried to think a bit.

He didn't sit long; he took his eats and walked over to Frenchy and went to where the mule skinners were digging for water. The men were in a hole, handing buckets and pans of water and others were carrying it away from the muck. Walters was there mumbling, "smart aleck rancher, thinks he knows everything."

J.J. wanted Buck to hear that; it made him mad. They were having enough trouble without him complaining. "If you want to get out of here, everyone has to do something good. Along the edge of the dried up pond there are reeds, pull some reeds for the horses—while the Indians are gone." J.J. walked away without another word.

The Frenchman was equally annoyed with Walters, but tried to ignore him. "While there is a lull in the fighting, why don't you bake some new bread? This is getting a little dry," Buck said.

Buck supposed he was getting a little bossy; the Frenchman left without answering, went back to see what Suzy was doing. He was always watching her. She had her patient leaning against an empty barrel, his scalp almost in place, one stitch at a time. Frenchy was not only interested in the girl; he and the scout had been together two previous summers, robbed by the Indians both times. But Frenchy told Buck, "It only takes one trip to make you rich."

The Frenchman was terribly disturbed by the fact that Suzy was engaged to "thees Garett fellow." He wondered if the rancher was good enough for her. Buck knew he wasn't or he would have made his real name known and put the Frenchman in his place. But he looked after her well; she needed that, but it all made Buck jealous.

Buck was lying down, half overcome by the wine, but he needed a little rest; a body can only tolerate so much. Then he heard the Frenchman mumbling in his beard, but his beard was very becoming.

"I do not think the fellow is—" He paused.

Buck was afraid he was going to put in an uncomplimentary word, but Suzy didn't give him time.

"Sure he is good enough for me," Suzy enthused.

"I know you make a fine wife. How do you know he make a fine man?"

"Thank you Frenchy. I like your high opinion of me." She smiled mischievously as she threaded a needle.

Frenchy was a good-looking bastard, long black hair, not a particle of gray. He carried two side arms like a real westerner; he caught on fast. He stood there straight, chubby, but muscular—a determined man.

The fact that Suzy was loyal to her agreement annoyed the Frenchman, no end. "Anyone who can live in this country and fight Indians must be brave and strong. I know he's young and handsome, he said so in his letter. And he must be young and truthful. I can't ask any more than that."

Buck was almost asleep, but he nearly choked as Suzy reeled off all his good points. That Nido had really built Buck up. What a washout Buck would be if she really knew. Buck wasn't even brave enough to make himself known.

The Frenchman didn't disturb Suzy in the least; she just sat there, all her attention on the scout, who took another drink every time Suzy threaded her needle.

'You know he desperately wants a wife, so you know he will love you," Frenchy said to Suzy.

"Yes and I could be just thrilled if it weren't for the Apaches." The wind was blowing strands of Suzy's pretty blond hair in her face and she had difficulty brushing it aside since her hands were sticky with blood, but she worked on tirelessly.

The men picketed their horses near the mud pond, close enough for them to nibble on a few reeds, but not allowing them to get stuck in the mud. The animals needed the moisture. Frenchy's mule skinners had quit digging after getting a few buckets of water, which they gave to the horses while they whinnied for more.

Any time the Indians eased off, the women spent time baking bread. The most plentiful thing they had to eat. There wasn't much wood, but it was tall cactus country and the men dragged in a few saguaro logs and chopped them up. One woman had a tin which she used over an open fire. Two doors flung open and it accommodated four loaves. Different women used the oven. When too many twigs were used, the fire blazed up and the bread burned black before it was done inside. When the fire died down, the bread dried out instead of baking. A happy medium was hard to come by. Buck kept wishing that Frenchy would bake some new bread, but he couldn't waste what he had. The Frenchman dipped his into the wine to soften it up; Buck was going to try that.

While Buck was standing around, he lifted up his shirt to see how badly the Indian had tickled his ribs. Blood had welled over the entire scratch and crusted over. As Buck prepared to tuck his shirt back into his trousers, the nurse lifted her head toward Buck with concern as she threaded her needle. "You've been hurt, sir."

"There are others who need attention a lot worse than me."

"I'll put some salve on it when I get through with this brave young fellow."

"I think that is right kindly of you," Buck said.

The Frenchman couldn't stop bellyaching about that Garett fellow.

"I think this Garett fellow be the devil, to bring to bring a fine young girl like you into this hell."

Suzy was stumped for a second, but when she recovered she was Buck's equal. "Then why did you come into this hell?" She pushed her needle through Bob's scalp. It was like repairing a pair of Indian moccasins.

Frenchy had a ready answer, "I came here to sell goods, buy buffalo hides on the way back, geet reech, marry a fine girl like Suzy." There was a pause as bitterness welled up in his throat. "I think when I meet this Garett fellow maybe we have a duel for the hand of Suzy Carver." He stood up brave and tall, fingering his side arms.

Buck didn't want to shoot the poor devil, so he was glad when Suzy said, "No Frenchy, I don't want any bloodshed. Frenchy, I think you would make a very devoted husband, but I'm already spoken for."

Buck was thinking, if he made himself known, she would have chosen Du Lac.

He wouldn't have blamed her in the least. He had heard enough romancing and drifted off to sleep. When Buck woke up, he was out of touch. Things changed fast when the Apaches were in control. He would remedy that; he climbed about a hundred feet up the side of the cliff and took a look with his scope into the Indian camp. They seemed to be set up for the summer. Willow shelters covered with whatever they could find. Fires were burning. They were always great chunks of meat, stray pack ponies. Another of our horses. Buck figured the horse belonged to the wagon train or the Frenchman. It got away looking for water. Indians liked horse meat better than cow. That was good for the ranchers; horses were for the most part too plentiful.

Buck lifted his scope again. There was Marques Colorado standing on the rim of the canyon looking back at Buck. He must have found a telescope in the wagon with the missing wheel. They had dragged it to their camp and taken all the supplies.

When Suzy finished sewing up Bob, she lay there resting for a few minutes. She knew Bob was in danger of losing his life if infection set in. It would be weeks before complete healing took place. There would be festering and drainage and the wound might smell. Now, with a nurse there could be healing.

"If you get well, I'll give you a kiss," Suzy promised Bob. He didn't perk up at the thought of a forthcoming kiss. If you don't get well," she paused to give him time to think.

The Frenchman walked outside the enclosure with Suzy; he decided she needed to learn how to shoot a gun to protect herself. He had her by the arm walking in Buck's direction. She didn't seem to mind in the least; but held her skirt high to keep it from brushing in the dirt. She was doing the talking; glancing over at the Frenchman as though she had known him all her life.

Marques Colorado climbed down to his camp and up on the wagon with his scope. He was learning how to work it. He adjusted the scope until he had the Frenchman in full view just outside the wagon camp. The Frenchman had his arms around Suzy, helping to support her. She held the revolver stiffly in both hands at arm length.

Marques Colorado was studying the wagon camp with a determined look on his ugly face. He found the new toy more interesting than a thunder stick. Then he zeroed in on the Frenchman as he took the shells out of the gun and handed it back to Suzy. Marques was beginning to need bullets desperately. The sun was out and his braves were still in camp; some were annoying John from time, but he took his toll. The lull in battle gave the wagon train members a chance to cook and time for a good nap.

Buck didn't say anything; he had to keep his eye open for sneaky Apaches, but they were getting easier to spot.

6

Mito came up the steep bank and stood beside the broken wagon. He looked up at the great chief in admiration, but there was only annoyance in the chief's facial expression as he stared down at Mito. Marques put the scope aside and climbed down. He took the shells and tried to load his rifle. When they wouldn't fit, he threw them on the ground. They were the shells the boy had stolen from Frenchy. Buck knew the chief was giving the boy hell because they wouldn't fit his gun; that was his way of expressing anger, otherwise he might have become violent enough to have poked the kid with his saber. The Apaches were gentle with their children, but once they were initiated into a brave, they took the full fury of adulthood.

Mito was numb from lack of recognition, but he didn't retire and sulk. He stood there socially taking his tongue lashing.

Finally he seemed to defy his elder. He reached down, took a hand full of shells and threw them in the air. They all fell in different directions, as if he were trying to tell the chief that no brave would die from those bullets. He was right. Buck shouldn't have allowed him to have them.

Buck liked the kid's style; he faced bravery standing up to the chief. He would make a good boss some day, having learned first hand how to be cruel.

The chief seemed shocked by the boy's boldness and stood up straight, but that was too difficult at his age and he sagged back to his loathsome posture. He picked up the scope again and started watching the Frenchman and the girl, plotting how he could grab all the supplies.

The chief striped himself to a loincloth—he looked remarkably solid for his age. The boy took the yardage wrapped around himself and threw it on the ground and stood there naked. He seemed to wish the wisdom of his father would wear off onto him.

The Frenchman still had his arms around Suzy, helping her to steady the revolver at arm's length as she aimed. He was drawing that lesson out unnecessarily long. Buck could almost hear the Frenchman, "Pull the trigger." Then the click and Suzy would laugh. It wasn't funny, but Buck was glad she was learning to shoot.

Marques Colorado climbed up on the wagon with the wheel missing. Buck guessed he was trying to figure out a way to outsmart the wagon train, as Buck was trying to outsmart the chief. By direct attack the chief was losing too many braves. He was a shrewd old bastard. Buck got Elena back. He should consider himself lucky; he still has his scalp.

Now that Marques Colorado had come south to plunder, he would be harder than ever to deal with. Marques' plan would be to take the supplies from all the wagons for his people for next winter. The chief kept his eyepiece turned onto the Frenchman and the girl. The next thing he would have in mind would be getting that squaw. Women had a high bargaining price. Buck knew he had paid through the nose for Elena—with no regrets—she had made his brother a fine wife.

The kid was standing on the ground. He felt out of place there alone. Marques handed him the scope; he anxiously climbed onto the wagon, then onto a box. Marques helped him adjust the piece to suit his vision. Tonight when everyone sleeps, Marques would try something to prove his superiority.

The damn Frenchman was still mumbling, "Sigh down Zee barrel. Line up zee target—an Indian is coming right at you."

Suzy pulled back a little, breaking the Frenchman's grip on her. "I don't want to learn how to shoot."

"In the west you learn to shoot zee gun."

"I don't think I could kill anyone, even to save my own life." Her hair caught up in a slight wind and her dress fluttered. Her face was a little flushed from the sun. She looked beautiful, and innocent Buck was afraid she wouldn't last long if that was the way she felt.

Frenchy said, "I no like to keel, but the Apaches take all two time, this time I get through."

"Third time's the charm." Even though Suzy was trying to be jovial, she did seem concerned about the Frenchman.

Frenchy put a shell in the chamber of the gun and handed it back to Suzy. He pointed in the general direction of the mountain where she couldn't miss.

"Pick up a rock." She did, while Frenchy admired her curves, well hidden behind fluffy white frills. She threw the rock into the air and with his revolver, Frenchy shot it down and sharp pebbles rained down on them.

"This time I get through and marry Suzy." Buck thought he was a persistent devil.

Suzy fired. It wasn't just the click of the trigger that time, but an explosion. Suzy dropped the gun and stood there, her hands shaking, but still pointed in the direction of the mountain. Finally she caught herself; she was a nurse and was supposed to be brave.

She turned to the Frenchman as he picked up the gun. "Frenchy. I'm flattered. I hardly know you."

Buck hated to admit it, but the Frenchman was a very likable young man.

The Frenchman put the shells back in the revolver and stuck it in his holster. "You know me better than this Garett fellow."

That hurt Buck. He was not living up to his duties as a suitor; that hurt too. Frenchy was right, but Suzy didn't know how hard Buck was trying to protect her.

"I have to get back and see how Bob is doing." She started back to the enclosure of the wagon train, little rocks followed in her wake. "He has a sister. If I not bring him back, she lose her mind," Frenchy called after Suzy.

Buck thought it more important to do something rather than imagining what Frenchy had to say. So he hurried down, following the two into the enclosure. Then Suzy giggled. "I promised Bob a kiss if he got well."

"Then he get well," Frenchy said with finality.

Buck went into the enclosure, wondering why the Indians were resting so much. Marques Colorado generally drove his braves without mercy. Buck figured he had something better up his sleeve.

When Buck got back into camp, the men had gathered around Frenchy. One of his mule skinners had just brought in the remains of the carton of ammunition that had been left a hundred yards from camp. The skinner had counted the boxes twice and found one missing.

"The specials won't fit any of the Indian guns," Buck informed them and that seemed to ease the tension. The rest of the shells are out there in the weeds; send someone out to pick them up." Buck hadn't made it clear what happened during the night, the less said the better so it didn't disturb the camp so much.

One of the mule skinners had a bucket, watering his horse. Even though the water was muddy, the animal drank it all. Buck supposed the mud might give him strength; there wasn't much of anything to eat near by.

"Frenchy, they need an empty barrel," Buck said. "So the water can settle. Then you can give each animal a gallon a day—we may save them if the siege doesn't last too long." Men were milling around; some didn't know what to do. The women had sense enough to sew up the battered canvas on their overturned wagons.

Suzy stood guard over her patients like a professional, cleaning and dressing wounds; she was quite a woman. The Frenchman had more sense than Buck wanted to admit. Had he been a mite younger man, he wouldn't have stood for the intrusion.

The Frenchman poured the last of a barrel of wine into buckets. Flies gathered around the sweet purple stuff, got drunk and fell in. Frenchy then covered the buckets with some of his muslin. A mule skinner knocked the top out of the barrels. They carried the barrel from the enclosure to the dried up pond, where a trickle of water seeped into the hole they had dug.

"The deeper you dig the more water you get," Buck informed the men working, but they were reluctant to crawl down into the mud again.

Buck went back to the camp and approached the Frenchman. He had decided to take advantage of the lull and bake some bread—about time, but shut his mouth.

Frenchy pulled a long leaf of tobacco out of a pouch and handed it to Buck with a pipe. Buck wadded the long leaf of tobacco into the pipe and lit it over the fire he had built, all the time wondering how they could get out of this mess. There was no need to send out another scout. He would never get back. And that would give the Indians an additional horse to eat. The Frenchman was smoking his pipe as he kneaded the dough in a huge pan, not bothering if a few shreds of tobacco fell into the mix. Buck was sipping a little wine to get the strong taste of tobacco out of his mouth. Finally Buck decided the long brown leaves were too powerful for him and shook the pipe out on the ground. He was out of chewing tobacco, so he took one of the smaller leaves, wadded it up and stuck it in his mouth. It burned his mouth a little, but it tasted good.

"Too bad the Indians didn't get one of your barrels of wine. If they all got drunk, maybe we could get out of here." Buck was desperate to do something.

The Frenchman thought that over as he greased a Dutch oven hinged together, then placed in a well formed chunk of dough. He seemed startled for a second. "Maybe it work." He was puffing on the pipe between his teeth and it was difficult for him to talk. "I no like to waste good wine on savages. I give it some thought."

While thinking of delivering a barrel of wine to the Indians, Buck didn't rest. Then there was Suzy to think about in the stagecoach by herself. The Frenchman felt at home sleeping between his enclosure of barrels. If he could get the Indians drunk, maybe they could fight their way out. The wine was the best concord he had ever tasted, and the Indians, scarcely ever having tasted anything sweet, would guzzle it like water.

The next morning Buck had a huge slice of French bread, then another, but he was still hungry; he was used to steak, something that would stick to his ribs.

The Frenchman had grown his own grapes and made wine, so he hated to part with any, unless it brought him a price. Or alleviated the situation the wagon train was in. "We give it a try." Buck was not sure it would work so he was glad he hadn't made the decision. They had to do something, the people were restless, pinned down in the hot sun, watching their animals paw the ground and whinny for water. Frenchy motioned to several of the drivers; they followed him to one of the inverted wagons forming the closed circle. They grabbed hold of the high side and lifted it upright.

The Frenchman was beginning to have a glimmer of hope. "Maybe we get out of thees yet." His men respected him; he was fair, and they respected him because they liked his decisions. "The oldest skinniest animal," he told the anxious men. It was too good to hope for, but they hurried around hitching up the team. Buck wasn't sure of the outcome. Marques Colorado was a shrewd devil. He bargained until you had nothing left, then he reneged on his promises.

The team stood waiting. "Now a barrel of my precious wine." This was truly the Frenchman's and he watched with pain as the men rolled a barrel over to the wagon and lifted it in. Frenchy added a new spigot next to the bunghole. With one swift blow of the hammer; he drove the spigot into the bunghole without losing a drop. With a brace and bit he drilled a small air hole in the top of the barrel, so the wine would drain out properly. They placed a dozen cups in the wagon. Frenchy took a cup and filled it. He handed the cup to Walters.

The troublemaker drank. The sour expression on his face turned to delight for the first time since Buck had met him.

"They won't be able to resist that," Walters remarked as he licked his lips. "Good thing we were able to join up with the wagons; we wouldn't have gotten anywhere with the Apaches."

The old coot's stomach stuck out as though he had never missed a meal in his life. He had said enough things critical; it was good and time he said something good. He was probably catching on. He no longer mentioned getting to California within the month. Like the rest of them, he just wanted to live.

One of the mule skinners jumped on the wagon and fastened the reins so the team would go in a straight line. He called back to the Frenchman standing in front of the anxious crowd. "Pretty good team you give the Paches." The Frenchman was silent. The wine was his food he didn't want to think about the two horses.

When the skinner jumped from the wagon, he gave the horse a swat on the rump as did the skinner on the other side. They were all dressed alike. Buck didn't take time to know who was who; there were too many other things to keep in mind.

Everyone stood and watched as the team plodded across the dry lands; there was sadness in knowing the animals were not riding horses and would be eaten by the savages.

"When they get drunk, we pack up and leave." The French-man slapped his two men on the shoulder. Buck listened to them talk; they were getting their hopes up too soon. They had to do something. The horses were getting weaker every day, and a drunk Indian was meaner than hell. It would take all the French-man's wine to get them all drunk.

The team passed what was known as guard rock, close by. There were no Indians in evidence at that time, so some of the more venturesome men walked out and swatted the horses on the rump to get them to quit nibbling on green bushes and to get them to move on.

One mule skinner walked over to Frenchy; his drab uniform was covered with mud. "Frenchy, we got half a barrel of water and it's kinda clear."

"Give the water to the horses, maybe a gallon."

The team marched in a straight line, occasionally plucking at tips of green brush. Their mouths were so dry that they had no taste for the dry clumps of grass. They marched slowly up a small knoll; they must have smelled water in the little creek below and broke out into a trot. They gained speed and were soon going on a dead run. Buck was watching, afraid they might run into a canyon and destroy themselves, and the barrel of wine. Buck could see the wagon about a mile away. The savages must have heard the jingle of harness and the rumble of the wagon, because about that time they came up from below, some on ponies and some on foot. They grabbed hold of the team from both sides and brought them to a halt. Then they swarmed all over the wagon like ants on a morsel of bread. The team settled down under control of the Indians; after all they had traveled hundreds of miles and were not easily disturbed by strangers.

There were no supplies in the wagon, so some of the Indians examined the harness, while others explored the barrel. Buck had his scope out and got up on one of the overturned wagons. He had to see the details. One brave in loin cloth turned on the spigot. He tasted the wine on his fingers, while the precious liquid ran on the ground. He didn't dare tell Frenchy; it would have been too much for his heart. "Hey they like the flavor," Buck commented. The Indian put his head under the spigot and began to drink. There were many cups in the wagon; they needed to learn how to use them. When the brave took time to catch his breath; a naked Indian filled one of the cups. Watching, Buck was beside himself. With a cup they were lined up to take turns.

The chief came up the bank; he didn't yet have his hair braided, and it hung in sheets of black, so it made him look like a witch. His face looked sour as it always did, but he was sure of himself, and he left no doubt about who was in charge or who was the chief. With the butt of his gun he knocked the cup from the hand of one of the braves; no matter that a finger might get broken.

"Fools water." He had never seen fools water before, but he knew what it was. He knocked the cup in the face of another brave who was gurgling happily. Then he was near the barrel. With a single blow from the butt of his rifle he knocked the spigot from the barrel. He turned and faced the lot of them. He was old and stooped and his face a mass of wrinkles, but his braves cowered before him. Buck with his eyepiece could almost hear him shout. "First brave who takes a drink gets shot like white man."

"This is a trick; fire water is no good for Apaches." Two braves dropped their cups to the ground and precious liquid poured from the barrel onto the patched earth. Heart sick, Buck lay his scope aside; he hated to tell the Frenchman or anyone of the wagon train what really happened.

Marques Colorado stood guard as the wine poured from the barrel. His braves finally unhitched the team and led the horses away, the queer harness still jingling. They were workhorses and looked too cumbersome to ride, so the chief passed judgment. An Indian crawled onto the back of one of the horses. It had never been ridden before, and reared up on his hind legs. The Indian held onto the harness for dear life. When the animal failed to dislodge the object, it settled down and started to run in the direction of the canyon. When it came to the edge of a cliff, it stopped suddenly and hurtled the Indian into a ditch. The animal would only be good for eating. "Make ready to eat," the chief said.

Buck climbed down from his perch and said to those watching, "Marques Colorado is too smart to allow the Indians to get drunk. He calls the wine, 'fools water.'"

The Frenchman had delivered a team of horses as food, and a barrel of wine had been drunk up by the parched earth. Everyone felt like hell, but didn't know what to do next.

Buck walked around the camp surveying the situation. Suzy was carrying a revolver. Buck was glad for her. She kneeled down beside the scout and dressed his scalp. There was fester oozing through the stitching, but she expected a certain amount of that. The scout looked pretty good to Buck. He was facing Suzy; he had been partially scalped from the front. He was carrying on a conversation with the nurse. "It's none of my business, but you can't go wrong if you marry Frenchy." He was right, but Buck thought it was none of his business,

"I'm already betrothed." That was what Buck called loyalty. Buck was ashamed of himself and was afraid to identify himself. She was not the least bit impressed by further proposals and she could have her choice of men.

"Just in case you do marry the Frenchman—make him settle down, instead of running around and getting robbed by the Apaches every summer."

Suzy said no more, but made sure that Bob was resting comfortably in a bed of yellow yardage from the Frenchman's supplies.

"When I get better, I want to learn you how to shoot that gun better." Suzy treated it like a stick of giant powder. "You have to learn not to be afraid of it; the gun won't explode."

The hot sun bore down on the people and their wagons cut off the breeze. It was like a giant oven within the enclosure.

Next to the canyon where the Apaches had assembled, the heat danced in waves. Only in the middle of the night was it comfortable. Buck was thirsty; he had already drunk his share of water. The Frenchman's wine made him more thirsty. They had killed a great number of savages, but the odds against them were still eight to one of their fighting men. John had taken his toll as he slipped up on them from behind the boulders.

It was the middle of the afternoon and the guard was sleeping. For some reason the second guard wasn't going on until evening, and no one had agreed to replace him. Buck had taken a liking to the young kid who was the most adventurous of the two. Buck used kid, but he must have been at least twenty, long blond hair and a stringy mustache. Everyone called him Son. It was easier than saying Anderson. He was tall and lanky and would spread out to be a hulk of a man, the Indians willing.

Son slept restlessly during the day, but was back at his favorite rock the first sign of darkness. He was even more alert after the missing box of carriages, if that were possible. The loss was slight, but it only went to show that the Indians had things going their way. They just wanted to get to the wagon train, to let them know that they could move in and out of their camp at leisure.

When dusk came, Buck was determined to put a stop to thievery at night. Anderson leaned against his rock; Buck only wished that the other guard was there to lean against the other side. The rock was about eight feet across, half of a much larger rock; it was almost flat on top. And stood about shoulder high. Son had his gun in hand and looked from side to side.

Buck sat on the dry ground about a hundred feet away from Son. Buck had a moonlight view, all the way to the canyon, where the night view dropped abruptly to the Indian camp. As it grew darker, Buck could scarcely see the guard. Then a shadow moved in the distance; Buck stood up for a better look, but it was only a bush that wiggled from an occasional gust of wind. Soon there was a noise, like the breaking of a twig. Son turned in the direction of the sound. By that time there was only darkness, with indiscernible shadows and rocks scattered at random. There was a click, the sound intensified by the stillness of the night and the late hour. Buck was glad it was a metal sound; the guard was ready for danger. Son moved to the front of the rock to better see if an unwelcome guest might be moving in. That must have been when the Indian moved in and slammed his hand over Son's mouth and plunged his knife into his belly. Buck didn't realize until it was too late that they had lost Son. His blood boiled. If that was the way the intruder wanted it, he would get the same treatment.

The Indian wanted to make sure everything was clear before he came from behind the rock. He sneaked around looking for a second guard. When he found none, he made a run to the circle of wagon. Buck was mad, his heart beat too fast—that had never happened to him before. The Indian stayed close to the rocks when he could find one, running, hiding. In his moccasins he was quiet, even in the dark when he couldn't see where to step. Buck moved out to the first rock; he was close to the Indian. As he passed, Buck stepped out in back of him and grabbed him with his hand over his mouth. He stuck his knife in his back and held the Indian until all life had gone out of him, then he left him slide to the ground.

There had been but one Indian the night before and Buck was hoping there would be only one tonight. But the way Buck pieced it together in the morning, Marques, the chief himself, not wanting anything to go wrong, had gone to Suzy's tent and slapped his foul smelling hand over her mouth.

7

*A*fter the burial of Son, they hadn't even reached the wagons when a lone Indian came riding in. Even at a distance his dress told them that he was a chief, the chief. He had a decorated lance in his right hand, his badge of authority. Some hundred feet away he stopped and with great boldness threw the lance so it stuck into the ground at a slant and stood there wiggling, the attached ribbons of various colors dancing in the morning breeze. The newly-appointed guard had his rifle leveled at the chief, but they all held their fire. Why? The Indians were lined up along the canyon rim in the distance, awaiting a signal from Marques Colorado to overrun the camp.

The chief spoke first, "Marques Colorado come talk peace." Buck walked boldly out in front and the Frenchman followed. Buck had dealt with the sneaky bastard before. By then they were backed up by all the men in the camp, but that didn't mean a thing as long as the Indians had Suzy.

Frenchy dropped his sidearms to show that he feared nothing, but stupid bravery wasn't everything. Buck held onto his gun for the unexpected.

"Frenchy talk peace—already know what chief wants."

The chief spoke with gruff authority; he had to upper hand.

"Chief ask big price," Frenchy said.

"Braves say woman make fine squaw, no want to give up, worth big price."

"Frenchy wants to see if girl is alive." Buck allowed the Frenchman to do the bargaining. He didn't have anything to bargain with.

Bob, the scout, got up, although Suzy had forbidden him to rise except of necessity. He had a gun in each hand and Buck considered him a little impulsive, the way he lost his scalp for an antelope. "Hold your fire," Buck said to Bob standing there leaning on his rifle, but Buck meant it for all the men ready for battle.

"Come see," Marques snarled. He turned his horse around ready to leave. They didn't expect to walk. The Frenchman ran to the corral and climbed on the nearest saddled mount and Prince came up to Buck expecting at least a drink of water, but there was none. The three of them galloped off in the direction of the Indians assembled along the rim of the canyon. The chief left his staff stuck there in the ground like a solemn sentinel and Frenchy's arms lay nearby in the sand to show his good intentions. Buck rode beside the Frenchman; neither of them spoke, yet Buck knew he was glad to have him along as Buck was glad to have Frenchy. Neither was afraid; life wouldn't be worth much if they didn't get the girl back.

They came to the wagon that had been sent down with the barrel of wine and the other with a wheel missing. Buck supposed they had dragged them in for wood; they were stripped of nearly anything that would burn. Some of the assembled Indians were mounted and others stood around with rifles or bows. Smeared with different colored paints, they looked solemn and ready for battle.

A short distance from them a large cotton wood limb was planted in the ground, its branches spread out like a cross. Suzy's arms were tied to the branches. Her hair was hanging in all directions and her face was crawling with flies. The morning sun had driven all the strength from her young body, causing her to sag so her whole weight was supported by her arms and she had not the strength to move. She was clothed in a single garment, the red night gown she had worn the night before.

When the Frenchman saw Suzy, he impulsively made a dash in her direction, but was saved from sudden death by the braves who surrounded his horse and grabbed the reins. They led the Frenchman back to where Buck sat, mounted, waiting for the bargaining to start.

Buck could tell that if the Frenchman had ever loved a woman, it had to be Suzy, but Buck was hoping he wouldn't lose his head. Buck could not say the same for himself; it was pity he felt for the girl. Buck had brought her here and he would be loyal to her as she had been loyal to him. She had rejected the Frenchman's offer of marriage. Buck would marry her if they both got out of there alive, only if she wanted it that way. Right now, it wouldn't be difficult for pity to be turned to love.

The Frenchman and Buck sat on their horses, surrounded by half-naked Indians; they were helpless in relieving the girl's sufferings. "I geeve my life for this girl, but when I geeve, I want her free," Frenchy said bitterly. Marques understood. That was what he had intended. But Buck knew Marques didn't give a hoot for the girl's life. He was losing braves from John's men entrenched in the canyon, creeping up behind rocks and picking them off, one at a time. They knew better than to claim any knowledge of the men in the canyon, so Marques was holding out for a quick deal.

"Marques no want life," he sounded innocent enough. "Marques only want supply goods, blankets, pots."

Buck looked at the Frenchman; he was the one who should start the bargaining.

"Frenchy have twelve wagons—he geeve all—I no geeve wagons, not mine."

The chief held up his hand as he spoke. "Bring one wagon at a time—braves unload next to squaw." He pointed to Suzy. She was his bargaining power.

"Frenchy breeng wagons—then girl go free."

"Everyone goes free or the Frenchman will not part with the wagons," Buck butted in and Marques Colorado nodded. Whether he meant it or not, Buck could not be sure. But Buck had more to say. "The girl you have there is a Medicine Girl; she can help heal your braves. You should not have her tied up like that." The Frenchman sat there astride of his horse, fuming at the way the girl was being treated so that every other word was in French, but he heartily approved of what Buck was trying to accomplish. Marques looked in Suzy's direction, but didn't seem impressed.

Mito, the young protégé, showed up in a yellow shirt with black polka-dots; his body bound tight. Marques was dressed the same. Frenchy recognized the yardage from his abandoned wagon and mad as a hornet, he dashed off with his horse at a dead run.

Mito looked up to his hero, chief and father. Marques sat there astride his horse, lording it over the boy. "You learn many things from Marques—how to make deal." He was not only a great chief, but an educator who could teach cruelty and deception.

"You are not going to give the squaw back?" the boy asked.

"Marques make trade—Marques keep word."

Mito stood there looking at the great chief, trying to deduce the sudden honesty of the one whose stature grew greater among his people every day. He didn't have Buck fooled, but what else could they do?

By the time Buck got back to camp, the Frenchman had already hitched a team to the first wagon. His mule skinners had started loading it with supplies. Up to that time the wagon had served as a barrier against flying arrows and bullets; an open space was left in the enclosure. "Not too full," he advised his skinners, still thinking he might find a way of saving some of his supplies, but Buck knew he never would. Buck was only wondering how to save the girl when Marques failed to honor his agreement.

"Frenchy make deal with the chief, if he say oui, geeve Suzy a drink of wine." He handed the mule skinner his hip flask; Buck was sure Suzy would never drink a drop of that wine.

Buck advised the driver, "We'll be dead ducks if you start any shooting." He looked at Buck as if he hadn't been around the west very long and tucked a revolver under his leather jacket. Buck understood. The Frenchman and his men upended another wagon and the people from the caravan started moving in to complete the smaller circle of wagons.

The Frenchman ate a slice of bread and drank a cup of wine. He handed Buck a cup, but Buck declined. It was food to him, but it only made Buck dizzy so he couldn't think. But Buck ate a slice of bread.

While the Indians were carrying the supplies back to their camp, the wagon train was relieved of the pressure of immediate attack. Buck didn't like the way the deal was going, but he had done the same thing when he bought Elena back from the s.o.b.

That was when Buck thought he should join John and his men. They were not part of the bargain and they planned to keep on fighting. When Buck rode in, they hadn't gotten organized yet that early in the morning, so he took charge. The vaqueros were good men, but needed a leader and Buck was closer to them than John; he worked with them. They all gathered around Buck. Some of them made their way up to side of the ravine to see what the Indians were doing. The women were carrying away the light items of booty and the heavy items were piled up beside the two wagons, waiting for the swarthy bucks to buckle down to the heavy work. They took their positions behind boulders and decided there were too many Indians for an out and out attack. As they restlessly waited, Buck lifted his field piece; the girl was still there tied to the cottonwood limbs.

Buck handed the telescope to Nido. "What do you think?" Buck asked, as Nido looked at the girl for the first time while the Indian women were milling around, each sorting out what they thought was the best pan or knife.

Marques Colorado sat stoically astride his horse watching his subjects with pride. This would be remembered as the year of plunder. No one knew what to do with plows.

Marques sensed his people's displeasure with the odd shaped pieces of iron. Buck knew he was shouting, "There will be more wagons." Indian squaws carried away bolts of colorful yardage and little children used cooking utensils as toys.

"The girl, what do you make of that?" Nido was coming to his senses.

"That's the mail order bride you ordered for me," Buck said bitterly, wanting to blame it all onto him. "I write for no more mail order brides." He continued to study Suzy through the glass lifted to his right eye. "She is beautiful. Don't forget there is the leetle matter of forty-eight pesos."

Buck liked the son-of-a-bitch, but all he did was get him mad, always talking about money.

There's very little the Garetts can't do when they put their mind to it. Seeing the girl suffer, Buck wasn't thinking of money and it reminded him never to get drunk again. Buck didn't think anyone would get into so much trouble as he did. He could take it, but that innocent girl. "We can't let that girl die hanging there while those bucks take pride in watching her suffer."

"What do you have in mind?" Nido asked.

"I don't know yet, but you're gonna help me. Think dammit! Think!"

They slid back down the side of the canyon and sneaked farther up the ravine, closer to where the Indians were carrying their booty to their tepees. One Indian was coming farther in their direction than the rest. He had pots and pans thrown over the rump of his horse; the noise made his animal jumpy and he lost control. He dismounted and pulled the pans from the animal while he held onto the rope he used as reins. Without the clatter of utensils, the horse quieted down, so the Indian sat down to examine his booty. He had a pocket watch dangling from a chain and held it close to his face. When he pushed the stem, the cover flew open and he jumped. That seemed interesting, so he tried it again.

Buck realized the Indian was engrossed in his toy, so he sneaked up on him like a cat after a bird. As Buck rushed up in back of him, he had a large rock in his hands. "I hate to do this, amigo." Buck came down with the rock on his head and stood there for a full thirty seconds, too stiff with tension to move. Buck pulled the jacket and leather trousers from the body. When Buck had dressed in his clothes, he was glad the Indian had worn more than a loin cloth. He led the Indian pony away and walked bravely back to Nido, concealed behind boulders.

"Don't just sit there and laugh," Buck scowled at him. "Get yourself an Indian. Get one with a horse."

"Do you think I would look funny?" He laughed some more.

"Maybe worse, Buck snapped." If he hadn't been Buck's friend and Buck needed him, he would have sent him home.

"Indians don't wear a mustache," Nido claimed.

Buck knew that, but he was an Indian just the same. If Buck was going to help the girl, it was now or never.

Buck walked bravely out into the open with a few pots and pans, the watch dangling from his wrist. Another Indian with pink yardage wrapped around himself rode by. He saw Buck playing with a better prize than he had. He was chewing on an enormous bone as he dismounted.

The Indian said something to Buck in Apache. Buck halfway understood, but he hung his head to conceal his whiskers and flipped the watch open. At first the brave was intrigued, then he stared at Buck as though he might be a stranger. Buck was the one who needed the yardage to conceal his mustache. His revolver was sticking out from under his short ragged jacket. Buck was afraid he would see it and become suspicious. Buck looked down at the revolver, wondering what to do and pushed the watch in the Indian's face. He quit eating and stared at Buck's whiskers. Buck pushed the stem of the watch, the cover flew open. The Indian jumped aside and Buck struck him a hard blow and he rolled into a ditch below. Nido was there waiting to dispose of him.

Buck picked up the bone to look natural. It helped to cover his mustache, but he refused to eat, even thought he was hungry. Buck could never go for eating horse meat and Nido laughed at him for being picky about his food.

Nido's Indian wore only a loin cloth, if you disregarded the pink yardage and Nido's skin was too white. Buck could have laughed under different circumstances. It wouldn't work, so they slipped down to the stream where Buck splashed Nido with mud and put a gob on his face to cover the mustache. But Nido's mustache was too long to cover; Buck had to sharpen his knife on a rock and trim it back while he squirmed from the pain.

By that time Marcos was dressed like an Indian, which meant most anything, if it was old and dirty enough, but with the unloading of the wagons, new clothes were beginning to appear— men in dresses and women in shirts, even suits of winter underwear became everyday wear.

Marques and Buck sat astride their ponies, but Nido's horse was a full-sized plow horse, probably captured from a wagon train and broke to ride.

"Shall we go?" Buck wasn't anxious to get into the stream of Indians, but he knew they had to, if they wanted to get close to the girl. Buck didn't yet know what they were going to do, but something was coming into mind. They were strangers and hoped to be accepted, since Cochise braves were beginning to drift into camp to help with the summer harvest of wagon trains.

Even though they were Cochise braves, they rode cautiously into the activity, where merchandise was piled every which way, not far from where the poor girl was tied up. Squaws and children were carrying away supplies in a continuous line, marching down a path along the hill to their summer dwellings covered with grass and reeds. The young bucks were taking their share of loot, to bargain for a wife. This would up the price of brides. In addition to the customary horses, the father of the bride would demand household goods. All he could get.

Marques Colorado was walking proudly around examining the loot. He wore a streak of spotted yellow cloth around his forehead to match the shirt he wore, unbuttoned, exposing his slumping brown chest streaked with grey. He had not always plundered, but he seemed to be enjoying it.

One of Frenchy's mule skinners was helping unload the wagons while a second, Dave, sat high in his seat with his leg in splints, outstretched as Suzy had ordered him to favor it. Dave could do little more than drive the team. He was there out of loyalty, but the girl was too far gone to recognize him or anyone else.

Frenchy had hoped to take Suzy back with him, but Buck was sure Marques would never give her up; that was the reason they sat there mounted and ready to ride. There would always be some little thing Marques wanted and that would delay matters.

The mule skinner in the wagon bed handed two rolling pins to an Indian woman. She took them eagerly; Buck had no idea why, maybe firewood. She was wearing a brown woolen shirt and her two boys in tow had on sack dresses. The mule skinner stared at them for a minute, then he called out to Marques. "We're supposed to take the girl with us." He didn't get down from the wagon bed, but pointed, while Dave sat there favoring his leg.

Frenchy was too impatient to depend on the mule skinners, so he rode in to make sure of the deal. Frenchy was determined and looked every bit as mean as the chief, but the odds were against him. Frenchy gave a long gaze at Suzy in her red gown, still tied to the stake, feeling, Buck was sure, as though life no longer mattered.

The three of them sat there mounted; they waited to see what might happen next. Marques had been informed that this was the last load. He was stumbling through the pile of goods throwing things every which way, using delaying tactics. The Frenchman rode bravely up to Marques; the chief didn't wait for him to speak first. "Marques look for bullets."

Frenchy knew it was useless to lie. "We do not breeng bullets." His face was red from the hot sun and the large glass of wine he drank with his meals, but he was determined to see this through.

"No bullets, no trade!" Marques folded his arms and stood straight for a moment, knowing he had the upper hand.

"You cannot keep zee girl tied up like zees," Frenchy waved his arms until his horse was frightened. "She is Medicine Girl, fix up braves." He pointed to Dave, sitting on the buckboard displaying his leg in splints and tied up with a white bandage.

Marques was not impressed. "We make deal." Marques began to flay his arms, which, as far as Buck was concerned, was a sign for us to move in for his protection.

Marques shouted back to Frenchy, "No trade—two braves decided to keep squaw." The old bastard should have smiled then, but Buck didn't think he could.

Frenchy and his two mule skinners were ready to mop up on the chief. But Marques didn't back down one inch, just stood there throwing his slumping chest out as dignity demanded. He knew the braves coming and going, and they would drop their loot at any time to back up the chief. That didn't include the three of them, but they were ready.

8

"Frenchy, it would be senseless to start trouble now," Dave called out, while waiting restlessly for the Frenchman. The girl in the red gown raised her head slightly and forced a look in the direction of her loyal supporters.

"Bring all bullets—Marques give squaw," the chief said in a tone that he hoped would convince the Frenchman.

"Eef I geeve all bullets—you would ask for all zee wagons from wagon train."

"Marques give word." The old bastard raised his hand to the sun overhead, as though he wanted the gods to witness his honesty. "Marques Colorado want French to come again when sun is long in the sky."

While Frenchy and the chief argued, the three rode in closer, as though they might help in case of a scuffle, but they headed directly for the girl tied to the cottonwood limbs. Marcos stopped on her left side and Nido on her right. Buck dismounted and with one concerted effort, pulled the post from the ground. Nido and Marcos each rested an arm of the cross in front of themselves and dashed off, the post dragging in the dirt. Buck mounted his pony. Marques was not the least bit disturbed as the rescue took place. He had promised the girl to Red Knife and it would be best if she had a chance to rest; she had accomplished her purpose. Frenchy could stand it no longer and dashed after the trio, but was instantly surrounded by braves who held his horse by the reins, while he shouted and shook his fist at the chief. "Marques not keep word." In his anger, Frenchy reverted to his native tongue.

Marques, a proud man, mounted his horse to be on the same level with Frenchy. He puffed out his chest like a toad and folded his arms, then he pointed to his braves with tommy-hawks and rifles. "Just try and get squaw back—we give her very nice home."

The two mule skinners were anxious to get away from the unruly Indians. "Let's go, Frenchy, while we're all in one piece." Dave whistled to the team and started to leave. Both men had their guns tucked under their shirts, but no matter how brave they were, it would be useless to use them, unless Suzy was back.

As Frenchy prepared to leave, "I get girl back." he shook his fist at the chief again, even though he was surrounded by braves. He gouged his horse in the belly and it shot out of the troubled area like a bullet.

At a sign from the respected chief, the braves did not follow Frenchy and his mule skinners, but allowed them to go free.

Some distance from the gathering of Indians, the trio dropped into a draw where they could untie the girl. She had passed out from pain and exhaustion, but when she woke up, she tried to strike back at them, but her arms were almost useless from lack of circulation.

When Buck kneeled down to cut the leather that had bound her to the post, he noticed the bark from the tree had rubbed one ankle raw. "We're not Indians, M'am. We came to rescue you." Buck tried to reassure her. "We speak good English."

"Apache not talk so good English," Marcos said, admiring the girl he understood Buck was supposed to marry.

"I have to trust someone," Suzy said wearily.

"Why don't you tell her who you are?" Nido said to Buck aside, while he looked over the prize they had just rescued.

"Not now. The way I look I might scare her, worse than the Indians."

Suzy was so exhausted she didn't know what was happening. They didn't have time to explain, but had to get out of there. They sat Suzy on Nido's horse where he could hold onto her. "I apologize senor, for taking the girl, but you have such a puny pony."

"Don't mention it. If we can't get to the wagon train, we have to get to John's camp." They looked over the knoll. The Indians were whooping it up for the moment, celebrating their victory. Buck didn't know where the safest place was, but some Apaches discovered the girl had been taken by the wrong braves. They had heard Red Knife was from Cochise's camp, so they didn't suspect Buck's trio as strangers, just yet.

Marcos understood a lot of Apache; he always claimed he was Mexican. Buck didn't doubt that, but Buck knew Marcos was part Apache. He told Buck the chief had given the girl to both Red Knife and Black Hawk.

If the chief had given the girl to Red Knife, there would be trouble. Red Knife was aggressive and he was definitely from Cochise's camp. Giving the girl to Red Knife was a good will offering that bound the camps closer. Really, Buck became Red Knife; Marques Colorado hadn't seen Red Knife in a while and he thought that Buck was Red Knife or at least a friend of Red Knife's; otherwise the rescue could never have taken place without a hitch.

There was always a boulder in the God forsaken area; from the top of one, Buck looked around to get his bearings. The Indians were whooping it up to celebrate their victory, but Buck knew he didn't have long to sit there and study the surroundings. There was a haze in the sky because of the heat, but Buck could guess about where the wagon train was and where John and his men were supposed to be. He should be out picking off Indians, but Buck didn't want that to include any of his men. Dressed the way they were, they were true Indians, but the mud over Buck's mustache had dried and was starting to peel off.

Buck was at the pile of supplies as several Indians rode in. The way the one seemed to be shouting at the chief, Buck supposed he was Red Knife, come to claim his prize. Buck imagined he had been busy carrying some of the larger articles to his wife and kids. He would be disappointed; after all he was a trusted brave from the land of Colorado. He would dare speak to Marques where others could not— "You promise, white-squaw to Red Knife."

Marques would be indignant and renege on his deal like he had with Frenchy. He would be angry the way Red Knife failed to hold him in esteem.

But, Buck thought Black Hawk rode in first, his horse in a lather. He had a lance in his left hand and stuck it in the ground, trying to act like a great chief. He jumped to the ground in a cloud of dust.

"Great chief promise white squaw to Black Hawk for finding wagon train." He wouldn't look the least bit shy the way he flailed his hands, but still trying to show respect for the leader.

The senile chief, in trying to please everyone, had forgotten some of his promises.

Buck scarcely knew Red Knife, but he was sure he had showed. He would be even more indignant than Black Hawk. The three would have it out. Buck could only imagine what they had to say. "Who deserves squaw, better than Red Knife?"

After his forgetfulness, the chief became the peacemaker. "Now is no time to fight over squaw. We have trade goods to haul into camp before white man takes it back."

The two seasoned braves failed to heed the great chief's advice. "Black Hawk deserves squaw, better than Red Knife."

"Too late, Cochise braves no give up squaw," Marques Colorado said to Black Hawk.

"I am Cochise brave, come to help rob wagon train," Red Knife growled. The three savages looked at each other; this was no time for jokes.

Black Hawk mounted his pony and shouted back as he dashed away, forgetting his lance, "Not too late. Death to Cochise braves who take squaw."

Red knife shook his first at Black Hawk and ran for his horse, a light reddish brown in keeping with his name. "Red Knife get squaw as promised."

The great chief looked weary for the moment, but he was as wise as Solomon when it came to dealing with disputes arising in camp. He would handle this in his own way, even if he had to do away with the girl to settle the argument.

Buck had taken too long sitting there on the rock watching and trying to think out his next move. He had sent Nido and Marcos on with the girl. They were already some distance ahead, raising a streak of dust in the direction of the wagon train. Buck would bring up the rear; that was the best thing he could do.

They rode northeast following a wash that led to the wagon train. Marcos' spotted pony labored under his weight, but it was not far back of Nido and the girl. He had his arms around her. Buck should have been carrying her on his pony, but the workhorse was more sturdy. Suzy was in good hands. Nido would protect her to the last, but Buck hoped he could get Nido back to his wife where he could brag to her about the rescue for the rest of his life.

The Indians were gaining on them now. But they were near enough to the wagons to see that Marques Colorado had not kept his word. Another band of about twenty Indians were bearing down on the camp preparing to circle it. It would be difficult to reach the wagon train without being shot at by both the Indians and the whites.

Marcos and Nido both brought their horses to a halt near

Buck. The Indians following them were closer. "What do we do?" Marcos asked.

"Maybe we not been living right," Nido ventured. He was always making wisecracks instead of thinking. Suzy looked wild-eyed, sitting there on the horse, her red gown pulled up and her bruised legs dangling. The horse had no saddle and it was foaming at the mouth from the long run. A workhorse was not meant for running.

"I can't say what's best to do, but let's drop down in this ditch and try and even things up for those poor devils in the wagon train," Nido said. The circle of wagon trains was much smaller and the settlers were in greater danger than ever. Frenchy had wasted his goods and Marques Colorado was determined to get everything the settlers had. Buck felt sorry for everyone except the rich dude who thought he could buy himself out of a bind.

Buck worked his pony to the edge of the bank. It was a five foot drop, but there was sand below. Indians ponies were used to rugged conditions and Buck coaxed his to jump and urged Nido to do the same. Soon as Buck hit bottom, he was off the horse and picked off an Indian up ahead as he rode through the ditch next to the wagon train where the banks had been worn down.

Nido's horse was not a native and refused to jump. Then Nido saw Red Knife and Black Hawk coming at breakneck speed. "We stay together," Buck shouted back to his people. "Get down in here." When Buck looked up again, there were four Indians raising a cloud of dust coming in their direction. Then Marcos and Nido with the girl veered away from the ditch. Buck had expected them to dismount and jump down to Buck, where they could fight it out. But they rode away from the wagon train instead. Buck knew they could never outrun the four Indian ponies. And he was right.

Buck was down in the eroded ditch, sneaking up on the shouting Indians riding around the wagon train. He was trying to get as many as he could before he had to turn and protect himself from the rear. Every time Buck shot an Indian, he looked back. Nido and Marcos were gone with the girl; Buck mumbled to himself, "I didn't aim to desert you."

Buck was taking his toll. The Apaches began wondering how their ranks were being decimated from two directions.

Buck sneaked closer to the wagon train; men were hiding behind their overturned wagons. They had good embankments of dirt. They were catching on.

The Frenchman was in back of his wine barrels. If a barrel happened to get punctured, he drove a peg into the hole immediately.

An Indian crossed the gully ahead of him. Buck took him in the chest. Buck had a good hiding place and he got every third Indian as they crossed the gully to get to the wagon train. They began to take notice something beyond their control was wrong.

Buck could have been proud of his luck, but he was sure by now that the girl had been captured again, and he didn't think she could take much more.

After the Indians suddenly rode back to their camp, Buck stood up and waved frantically. "Hey! It's me, Buck. Don't shoot." But a bullet came his way. He went down groveling in the sand for protection. He took his Indian jacket off, stood up and waved it. His skin was so white, no more bullets came and he slowly walked toward camp, holding his rifle over his head.

The Frenchman came out to meet Buck and gave him a big hug. "I theenk you be dead." They made a run for it in case there were Indians hiding in the rocks. Buck knew there were still Indians on the other side of camp, not too far away for a good shot with the proper rifle.

Everyone was glad to see Buck and he told the Frenchman about the girl. He offered a change of clothes, but Buck asked to use his razor instead. Buck hoped he would be the only real Indian most of them would see close up. Everyone swarmed around him.

"I'm going back out there soon as I shave off this mustache and get a slice of your bread, Frenchy."

Walters was standing there in a different suit of clothes, his belly as round as ever. He was trying to look on the bright side. "Maybe we'll get out of this yet." Buck didn't know why he said that.

The Frenchman glared at him. "We'll never get out of here until we get Suzy back."

Walters mumbled, "She won't be the last girl captured by Indians."

Buck would have slugged him for that, but the Frenchman did it for him. Buck got in between the two of them. "We haven't got enough men to fight the Indians, so let's knock it off."

But to Walters, Buck said, "You don't have to act so cold; she was to be my wife, I'm Buck Garett."

Walters didn't say another word but slouched away. Buck knew the Frenchman thought a lot less of him; Buck was the one who had brought her into this hell. The Frenchman couldn't have felt any worse about it than Buck did. The Frenchman brought Buck a large glass of wine, a generous slice of bread, his straight blade razor and a glass of water to shave with.

"If I'm to live an Indian, I should look like one." Buck was in a hurry to get back out there and look for the nurse. Everyone said Buck was a fool except Frenchy; he said he was the fool. Instead of putting the water on his whiskers, Buck drank it.

The stagecoach driver thought it was time to survey the situation. He climbed up in the driver's seat, the highest spot in the camp and looked around.

"How is the water supply for the animals?" Buck asked the Frenchman. He wanted him to know there was no hard feeling the way he felt about Suzy.

"We get a trickle. We have someone dipping when it is safe."

"Enough to keep the animals from dying?"

"We just water zee strong ones."

That told Buck more than he cared to think about the animals.

At that moment, an arrow came flying through the air and took the stagecoach driver square in the shoulder. He fell to the ground. A harassed looking woman, her bosom hanging low in her sack dress, came screaming, "We need Miss Carver." She grabbed the coach driver's gun out of his limp hand and fired a shot at random. Then she stood there bent over the coach driver looking raving mad.

"Nothing will help him," Walters shouted at her. He knew his hopes of getting to California were growing slimmer.

Frenchy's scout stuck his gun between the spokes of a wagon where he rested it. The Indian had lingered too long as he looked from behind the rocks. Bob dropped him and started to reload. The bandage on his head was dirty, and his face was red as though he might be running a fever. He leaned the gun against the wagon and lay back down ready for the next Indian.

Buck finished shaving, but his face hurt. It felt as if he had dug every whisker out by the roots. Buck should have used some of that water for shaving instead of drinking it all. But as he a looked into Frenchy's broken mirror, Buck knew he could better conceal his identity; his face was bloody as though it had been painted with red ochre. Buck went to say hello and good-bye to the scalped scout. He didn't have time to hang around. He was chewing on his slice of bread; it tasted good even without butter. Buck was afraid to sit down after the glass of wine. If he started to relax he might not be to get up again.

The Frenchman had coaxed the half-demented woman down under the protection of one of the wagons. He got her a cup of wine. She didn't want to become addicted to drink, but he was so confident that it would help her relax that she drank it all. The woman was determined to carry the coach driver's rifle around with her.

"Do you know how to shoot?" Frenchy asked her.

"After what I've seen, it just takes determination," she shouted to everyone.

If they didn't have some kind of relief soon, she was afraid she might lose her mind. Buck learned later they had buried her husband the week before.

"It do no good to shoot eef you do not aim. The kindness of the Frenchman would be good for her. "I weel show you how to aim."

The Frenchman put his arms around the woman, showing her how to sight down the barrel, but Buck knew he wasn't enjoying it the way he had when he instructed Suzy.

Walters was still as sure of his opinion as ever. He walked over to the Frenchman. "I have a white handkerchief; shall I wave it to surrender next time the Indians come to attack?"

"You do and zee Apache shoot your head off," Frenchy told him.

"They are that cruel," the woman said. She was in shock, hadn't slept in forty-eight hours and brandished her rifle in Walter's direction. Frenchy took it away from her, and Walters walked away as though nothing had happened. People from the east had no knowledge of how the Apaches lived; they grew up knowing no other life than savagery. They had no pity on their captives, except children.

Frenchy finally coaxed the woman into drinking another cup of wine. That was his cure-all as well as food, better than the medicines Suzy had in her satchel. The woman's knees buckled under her and she lay down in the shade and went to sleep.

Buck thought it was about time he got out of camp; he was tired of listening to the petty bickering. He had a woman to rescue. Buck had no real fear for Suzy's life, but that was the worst part of it. They did away with the men not the women. They might try and trade Nido and Marcos for cattle from the ranch, but that was not likely. They would probably keep them until they had more time to enjoy torturing them, hung upside down over a fire.

Buck took the saddle off Prince and used a single rope instead of a bridle, which seemed to be Indian style here at the moment among Apache braves. Frenchy hated to see Buck go, but he knew he was set on saving the girl. Buck knew Frenchy loved her, and he couldn't blame him. She was too young and good for Buck, but he figured Jewell would take to her like a fly takes to honey. Buck was a real Apache as he broke away from those gathered round him and rode out on Prince.

Buck headed directly toward the two wagons that stood along the crest of the canyon. He was weaving Prince around one of the larger clumps of brush when a young Indian jumped up from the shade. Buck was set on drilling him, but he noticed the Apache was limping when he reached up toward Buck. A cartridge had taken him in the left foot and he wanted a lift back to camp. He wore one high-topped moccasin, but the one for the left foot had been removed and he carried it in his hand. He showed Buck his foot as he favored it, then the moccasin with a nasty hole in it. He looked so young and innocent, probably his first battle with the whites. Buck reached out and grabbed his arm. Prince stood still and Buck swung him up in front of himself were he could stick his hunting knife between his ribs any time it became necessary.

The young man expected to recognize Buck and turned around for a better look, but Buck pointed him in the direction he was going. Buck knew a few words in Apache and Buck said, "Cochise." Buck said he didn't think he knew many Cochise men.

When he saw the dry blood on Buck's upper lip, Buck let him know he had been wounded and couldn't talk. Buck pulled one scab off and fresh blood ran down his lip. The young man bought that and they got along just fine. In camp, he helped conceal Buck riding out in front. He did all the talking and was excited about the white girl they had captured. He was young and would have been glad to have her as his squaw even though he hadn't seen her, but he could imagine how beautiful she was. He knew he didn't have a chance, the older men would fight for her and Marques Colorado owed them favors. That was the jist of what he had to say. Buck kept his mouth shut or he would have known he was white; then Buck would have had to stick his knife in his back. As much trouble as Buck had with the Apache, he still hated to kill one, especially one who hadn't quite grown up.

A few women and children were still taking supplies to their camp, and the pile had grown small. There were heavy items that they had no use for—a steel bedstead, a cook stove, several lengths of black pipe, and plows. Some women were tired and had taken time to loiter and examine the strange booty. Others were going down the hill for the last time to prepare new clothes from the various bolts of colored yardage they had a squirreled.

The sun was hanging low and Buck wanted desperately to find where Suzy might be before dark. They climbed down; the bank was steep. Using only one rope instead of a bridle left Prince confused and Buck had a hard time guiding him, so he got down to lead Prince. Buck let the young brave ride; that way he knew he would have one friend in camp. Once down in the canyon, Buck headed for the greatest number of shelters. He shouldn't have too much trouble finding Suzy if she still had her red gown on. He kept his eyes open. The Indians were eating well, they had a barrel of flour in the middle of his path and women were dipping out of it. Buck was not sure they knew exactly what to do with the flour. Nor did he know how to get Suzy out if he found her. But he was feeling braver all the time. It was getting cooler so he could wrap up tighter. That gave him added protection. Buck was toting a rifle he could use as a jousting stick if necessary. He didn't dare fire the thing. That would alert the whole camp and that would be the end of everything.

Meanwhile, Nido and Marcos were carrying on a foolish conversation instead of plotting how to escape. They had allowed Suzy to be taken without them being disposed of.

"I wonder why they not keel us yet," Nido pondered. That was the last thing Buck wanted to think about. He had too much to do before they got him.

Then Marcos said, "I see no reason they not keel you. Me, I am veery important ransom. For me they will ask many cows and John weel geeve them. There ees no reason why they not keel you."

Nido seemed to think that was sound reasoning so he changed the subject. "Buck—he didn't want the girl to know who he was. I thought he was serious when he asked me to order heem a bride."

While the two, Red Knife and Black Cloud, slapped each other about, Marcos squirmed to free his hands, but to no avail.

"What are we going to do with the girl if Buck doesn't want her?" Nido asked.

Marcos looked at Nido for a moment.

"Shut up! I want to hear what the braves have to say." Buck couldn't understand everything, but a third party had the girl until matters could be settled. He expected the two braves to kill each other, then the prize would be his.

"What are we going to do about the girl?" Nido kept asking, until Marcos told him to shut up again.

Buck was now down on the ground where he could wait for things to come to a head, he pretended he was wounded and needed to rest, which he really did. Buck had a rag across his mouth as though he had been injured. It helped to conceal him better and he wouldn't be expected to talk. Frenchy's straight blade was more like a sword than a razor and his face felt as if it were wounded, injured.

9

When Buck raised up, campfires were flickering throughout the valley. Smoke filled the air and he was drowsy, but he didn't dare sleep. He kept one eye open. Then Suzy came staggering near the path where he lay. She was prodded by a fat Indian woman and they both carried a bundle of twigs. Suzy was utterly exhausted, her hair tangled and her face dirty. She dropped the wood next to a shelter and fell down beside it. If she wanted to escape, it would have been impossible in her condition.

The sun was a beautiful red over the horizon but the day's work for the Indian woman wasn't over. The squaw went into the brush shelter and came out with a heavy urn and two new water buckets. She gave Suzy a yank, brought her to her feet and placed the heavy urn on her head. Even though the Indian woman was sturdy looking, she carried the two light buckets.

The Apache squaw hadn't been in charge of Suzy for very long because she had just then introduced herself. "My name Jhilta, what you?"

"Suzy," the poor girl was too exhausted to say anything more. Jhilta pushed Suzy ahead of her down the slight incline toward the stream. Suzy could scarcely stagger, but Jhilta shoved her along and Buck followed at a distance.

Although the Indian woman seemed glad she had a slave, she still hated for her husband to have a second wife. "Pretty Suzy should be glad."

As Suzy stumbled down the stony riverbed, she had to make a special effort to talk, but hatred for the situation made her express herself. "Glad to be in this stinking hole?" she scoffed.

Even thought Jhilta was envious of the blond girl, she was too much of a savage to understand why Suzy shouldn't be happy. "Glad three braves want you for a squaw?"

Suzy looked at Jhilta in bewilderment, tripped over a rock, dropped the urn and broke it into a thousand pieces, and fell to the ground. If Suzy was frightened, she didn't show it, but seemed to feel things couldn't get much worse. Jhilta slapped Suzy across the mouth before she had a chance to get up; then she put both water pails into her hands.

Buck would have stepped in and taken Suzy in his arms, but he knew they would never get out of the camp alive. Then Buck wanted Nido and Marcos along. If the Apaches found the girl gone in the morning, they would tie the two men to a stake and have their fun.

"I don't want a brave," Suzy almost sobbed, but she didn't have strength enough while she struggled to her feet.

"My brave, big fine man—he fight for you."

"What is he going to do with you?"

The Indian woman didn't answer, but Buck knew Suzy would carry water, find wood and gather seeds.

"Why don't you let me escape, then you could have your brave all to yourself."

That went over Jhilta's head, but she would be happy to have the new wife do much of the work.

When they arrived at the stream, Suzy threw her buckets down, dropped to her knees and drank for a long while. She splashed water in her face and washed her hands and arms. As she rose up, Jhilta put a full bucket in each hand. When Suzy lost her balance going up the grade, Jhilta pushed her forward. Suzy was young; Jhilta hoped to get a lot of work out of her.

After a hard day in the sun, it was a time of leisure for the Indian men, but for Buck the anxiety never ended. More campfires were burning. Buck came onto Prince; he had eaten and had his fill of water. Buck tied him up where he would be ready when he needed him.

Red Knife and Black Hawk had now come to blows. That was good. When they wore themselves out, Buck would step in. Black Hawk didn't dare shoot Red Knife for fear of Marques, but he struck his foe with his powerful fist and knocked him over. Red Knife raised up on his elbows and a fiendish scowl spread over his face. He sprang from the ground with his knife in his hand, but his opponent stepped aside. They shouted at each other; they slashed out with their knives, each dodging the other's blows.

Suzy and the Indian woman were inside their shelter, both leaning against the stiff buffalo hide wall. Jhilta already had Suzy weaving a basket of soapweed reeds. But Jhilta became excited by the noise of the men fighting; it brought back memories of when she was young and was wanted by more than one man.

Jhilta shoved Suzy outside to witness the show. It seemed that the Indian girl had taken a liking to the blond haired stranger, but she probably only wanted her as a workhorse.

"What are they fighting for?' Suzy asked.

That also went over Jhilta's head, but Nido called out to let her know he was still around, "For you." His wrists were bloody, but he sighed. He could tell even an Indian girl hated to see the passing of her youth. Suzy sank down and closed her eyes in horror. Instead of hating Suzy, Jhilta felt excitement for her. She spoke Apache and Buck understood enough to know how she felt.

Marques Colorado knew that Red Knife and Black Hawk were still wrangling over the girl. He was a man of knowledge, but not necessarily of justice. He was looked up to by his braves because of his ruthlessness. He strode to where the two men were fighting and stood bravely in between them, daring either to touch him. He shouted at them to stop their fighting, but neither stopped trying to punch each other. It wasn't safe for children near the fight, but none came close to the two as they struck out.

"If you can't decide peacefully who is to get the squaw, she must die," Marques shouted for everyone to hear.

That was a blow to those who understood Apache. "What did he tell them?" Suzy asked Nido, but he did not answer while Marques was around.

The angry braves put their knives aside and the great chief left, but he would be back if the two did not heed his warning. There would be hell to pay.

Finally Nido called over to Suzy, "Great chief say—eef braves can not decide peacefully who get Suzy, then Suzy must die."

Suzy had already learned to tuck one reed under the other, the rudiments of forming a basket. She gave a little sigh, bowed her head and dropped her bundle of reeds to the ground. Then as she thought it over, "Maybe it would be better that way."

The two Indians took their chief seriously, but stood there scowling at each other. The fight was over, so Jhilta took Suzy back inside. Her tent was a neutral home until a decision could be made. If the Cochise Apache and the Marques Colorado Apache killed each other, so much the better; her husband would get the girl and Jhilta would get all the work out of her.

As Buck walked bravely about the camp, biding his time to escape with the girl, he scrounged up a big chunk of meat. Like he said, it was against his principles to eat horse, but a body has to have something to maintain strength, and after a time anything tasted as good as it smelled.

Since Buck was a Cochise brave, he wasn't really recognized, but tolerated and left alone. Buck moved about while Indians appeared and disappeared like ghosts in the semi-darkness and Buck was one of them. But he intended to be out of the camp by morning; he couldn't take the pace any longer.

With the loss of Suzy as well as his supplies, the Frenchman was beside himself. A lesser man would have greased his wagons and headed for St. Jo where he had outfitted his supply train or gone back to hoe his grapes. But the Frenchman was determined to do something more. He encountered danger that he forbade his men to enter into. He picked up one of his Sharp rifles, destined for a trading post, climbed onto his riding horse and headed for the arroyo, where the Indians were favoring their wounds. He would look for the chief himself, dressed in the yellow polka-dot material too expensive to be wasted on the Indians, and he would look for a girl in a red gown. When Frenchy came to the brink of the canyon, he tied the reins of his mount to a chaparral, stole through the brush and secured himself on a shelf at the rim of the canyon. Then with his scope, he looked for an important Indian. He soon located the yellow cloth. He didn't take time to see if it might be the chief; he was mad and intent on revenge for the loss of the girl. If he killed them all, it wouldn't even things up.

There was the s.o.b. standing by the fire where meat was roasting. The chief was the hero of the day, admired by all his braves and looked up to by all the young girls. He had turned the Indian's poverty into riches. He let everyone know he had been into the camp of the enemy, a great feat for a chief his age.

The Frenchman was burning with rage; he didn't take the time for a second look with his scope. He lifted the sharp rifle and it shook in his hands. The distance was more than a thousand yards and it was growing dark. He steadied the heavy weapon on the limb of a tree and drew a bead on the yellow material that stood out in the gloaming. An Indian girl got in the way; one of his admirers. There were more girls; they swarmed around the chief. Frenchy waited. He wanted to get the important bastard; he didn't want to kill any of the women. He waited impatiently as it grew darker. When a girl, who stood in the way, stooped down to turn a slice of meat on the fire, Frenchy slowly squeezed the trigger. The heavy Sharp kicked his shoulder like the hind foot of a mule, but the Apache in yellow cloth threw up his arms and fell next to the fire, kicking as though he were dying.

Over a pipe of Frenchy's strong tobacco and a cup of his wine, he told Buck this was the way it had taken place. But he had not shot the chief, but the young lad, Mito, the chief's favored son.

After a time, the young brave stopped kicking and got up, grabbed his shoulder and went into his shelter where his mother helped him lie down.

The young girls who had doted on the boy ran screaming in all directions and went back to their shelters for the night. Frenchy only intended to hit the chief in the shoulder. The way it turned out, that was better for bargaining than death. Marques had to save the young kid's life.

When several braves started up the hill in pursuit of the enemy, the Frenchman's rifle belched twice and two figures clad in his supplies fell and rolled back down the bank. He scanned the camp for the red gown, but all he could see were the fires that dotted the valley and their smoke that added to coming darkness. The Frenchman left his perch on the side of the cliff and galloped back to the safety of the wagon train thinking he had shot the chief. That was only partial justice as far as he was concerned.

Marques heard the shots and tried to take charge of the nuisance. He was annoyed by the screams of the young girls echoing through the camp and found Mito writhing in pain and two medicine men were already chanting over him. He stared at his beloved son for a brief second, then nearly went berserk. He soon had the whole camp running around in circles.

Marques had no trust in his medicine men; they shook their rattler in vain. And it had not yet soaked in that the captured girl could be of any use. He hurried back to the other end of the camp where he would blame the trouble on Red Knife to his face, then Black Hawk. "Enemy shoot Mito," he shouted at the two of them.

Red Knife and Black Hawk didn't dare strike back or defend themselves in any way. When the chief had spent his fury on them, he hurried back to the lad; the two braves grabbed their weapons and ran in the direction of the trouble to try and be of some help.

When the commotion reached Buck's end of the camp, Jhilta hurried out of the teepee, leaving Suzy who had the partially completed basket in her hands; it was too dark inside to weave, but the Indian woman prodded her on.

Then a ragged, dirty-looking Indian girl went inside the shelter where Suzy was almost asleep. The girl went over and put her arms around Suzy. "I come as a friend," Buck heard her say. She had a Spanish accent.

Buck decided it was time to make his move, untie Nido and Marcos; soon as the girl left, he would grab Suzy. With all the excitement, there would never be a better opportunity. Buck walked around and kicked a little dirt on the closest fire to add to the darkness. When he came back, he saw two Indians wallowing in the dirt in mortal combat. He picked up the lance Red Knife had left, prepared to dispose of the troublemakers. Two more Indians hurried toward the commotion with food in their hands. That was when Buck decided that two Indians wallowing in the dust must be Nido and Marcos. Nido was chewing on the thongs that bound Marcos' hands, trying to untie them. "I hope that leather tastes good." Buck had his knife in his hand, ready to cut the leather.

"Tastes like hell," Nido gurgled.

Buck pushed him aside and cut the thongs. In minutes he had the two free. The girl with the red gown came out of the shelter and took a piece of meat back into the tepee. Buck wanted to grab her, but he wasn't quite ready.

"I didn't expect to see the two of you alive," Buck said. Marcos was trying to make himself believe that sometimes he didn't have any more brains that a ten-year old.

Most of the camp had gathered around the two braves who had lost their lives; the rest were trying to help the young kid. They needed Suzy, but they weren't going to get her, even if they did recall she was the Medicine Girl. The noise in the camp died down as Marques gave a speech, denouncing the wagon train anew, but that would have to wait until morning.

Buck moved slowly in back of Suzy. She was leaning over the fire, ready to pick up another choice piece of meat. Buck could have eaten more, but they didn't have time. It was then or never. He tapped the girl on the shoulder from the back. "We came to get you." She let out a scream. Buck guessed she didn't recognize him, so he slapped his hand over her mouth and carried her away while she kicked. Buck tried to assure her, "We came to rescue you." He expected her to recognize him; but he did look like an Indian, especially in the dark.

Marcos and Nido each grabbed a leg and they hurried away from the campfires and into darkness. Buck talked to Suzy quietly. "I'm Buck Garett. You're supposed to marry me, if you don't think I'm too old." Buck was sure Nido was pleased; he thought Buck didn't want the girl. Now he would get his forty-eight pesos. That was all he thought of—dinero.

Buck gave a short whistle; Prince whinnied and they went over to where Buck had tied him. He wanted a tidbit of something sweet, but wasn't going to get anything unless they got back to the ranch.

"I'm sorry to say I had to keep my greasy hand over your mouth, but I don't want you to let out another scream," Buck said. When they were far enough from camp that Buck thought it safe, he took his hand away and she lashed out at him.

"You're just as bad as the filthy Apache scum."

"You got me all wrong; I may have a little fun now and then, but I want you for my wife as we agreed." Then Buck realized the girl had a Mexican accent and her hair was dark. "Hey! I thought you were Suzy."

"It's the smoke from the campfires," Nido tried to reason.

"Shad up! If you can't be sensible." Sometimes Buck thought Nido was a little off his rocker.

Finally the girl explained, "I traded dresses with the other girl; they were going to kill her anyway." She had been living with the Indians so long, she sounded as calloused as they did.

"Not if I can help it," Buck said as he stared into the darkness. The camp was beginning to stir like a hill of red ants. Buck didn't think they had missed Suzy yet; they were too excited about someone brave enough to approach their camp at night and shoot two braves. They would take their anger out on the prisoners come morning. By that time, the girl was glad to be rescued and went along willingly, but it was too late to go back for Suzy.

"Did you bring any horses?" That was one of Marcos' silly questions. He'd been tied up by the Indians all this time and didn't know they were in danger.

"Horses! I'm lucky Prince hung around during all the ruckus. Let's get out of here. Nido, you run up and help those poor devils in the wagon train. Come morning, they're gonna need help—and dig another hole to water the animals. Prince was pawing the wet dirt on the side of the mountain. Dig there. Prince has a lot of horse sense."

"How do I get there?"

"Walk! On second thought, if you expect to get there in one piece, you better run."

Buck climbed onto Prince and the girl brought herself up behind him. Prince started up the path that angled along the side of the canyon and the girl held on like glue. Prince was taking his time. Buck thought he resented the long day, but Buck gave him a little tap on the rump and he climbed out of the canyon at a fast clip. Nido hurried toward the wagon train. Marcos traced the clatter of some pans and found a pony tied up for the night, still loaded with loot.

He followed; the utensils made a terrible noise. "Throw away those pans," Buck said as loud as he dared. It took a long time before Marcos complied with the order. Buck thought he was hoping to use them to buy an Indian girl. That might be more fashionable than lassoing one. He finally got rid of everything but the granite coffee pot; by itself it didn't cause a clatter.

When they moved out onto the flatlands, Marcos had a lot to say. He had been tied up for several hours and had listened to all the gossip by the Apaches. Cochise's men had moved into the canyon and planned to take John and his men come morning.

That was good to know, but morning was a long ways off and a lot of things could happen between now and then. The main camp of the Apache didn't mount up to follow, so they were reasonably safe for the moment. Buck allowed Prince to walk; it was better that way. Running at night, he might step into a hole and throw both of them into a heap of cacti. "Good luck," Buck said to Nido as he headed off in the night. "It's about a mile up there. Tell the Frenchman Buck sent you and he'll give you a good drink of wine."

Then Marcos told Buck, "Mito has been shot, badly wounded—a bullet through the shoulder, made it useless." It was then that Buck decided that they had gotten out of there just in time. If Marques could remember, he would come and get the Medicine Girl to help the boy.

It would be sometime before they came to the canyon where John and his vaqueros were camped. But according to Marques, Cochise's men were now on both ends of the canyon, surrounding him. That might pose a problem if they dropped back down again.

The girl was really appreciative of getting away from the Apaches. She told Buck what had happened. "With the red dress, I wanted to be the envy of the Indian women."

"But it was only a night gown," Buck tried to tell her. Her name was Amada. In Spanish Amada means "the loved one." Buck knew somewhere there was someone who cared for her.

The Apaches didn't know the difference between a night gown and a dress. Anyway, Amada was captured by the Apache nearly a year ago—when the wagon trains were going west.

Amada was in good health. She had her arms around Buck as they traveled. She held on like a vice and wore nothing but the thin gown and her muscles were as hard as steel bands, but that didn't say much for the life she would be forced to live when she was considered a woman.

"My clothes were nothing but rags," Amada explained. "I had a bolt of cloth, but not even a cactus needle to make a dress. The white girl had this beautiful gown—a shiny red. Marques Colorado was going to have her put to death, because no one could decide who was going to get her."

"But she is a nurse; she could be useful to the Indians if they could understand that." Buck needed to find out all he could about Suzy. Come morning, when the ant hill awakened, he had to start looking for Suzy again.

"She didn't feel badly about dying after I told her it would be better than living. She only regretted she couldn't do something for the wounded, even though they were Apache."

"You said her name was Suzy. Well, I took off Suzy's dress. I thought it would be a shame to have the pretty dress destroyed, but I gave her my old rags, so she would have something to wear. She lay there on the floor of the shelter weeping, too sad to put on my old clothes. So I helped her dress, but before I left the shelter, her eyes suddenly lit up in the dark.

"With these clothes, I can escape," she said.

"I told her she would die in the desert. She was too exhausted to go any place. I tried to tell her the best thing to do was to settle down and live the way the Indians expected her to. But I went out to the fire and took her a huge hunk of meat. I told her the best time to leave would be during the excitement. Then I left the tepee and was going to take some meat to a brave."

By that time Amada had told Buck everything. With the Indians below, it might be time to drop back into the canyon. There was too much to think about and Buck grew weary from lack of sleep.

10

Marcos took the lead as they dropped back into the canyon. He had grown up around here, speaking both Spanish and Apache and finally English. One horse snorted and two Apaches suddenly rose to protect the path into the canyon. They didn't call out to decide whether they were friend or foe, but discharged their arrows in the direction of the horse's hooves, striking the rocks. Buck left it to Marcos to let them know they were Apache. They spoke Cochise dialect and he spoke Marques Colorado variety. Buck couldn't tell the difference, but a few peculiarities had crept in. They knew Cochise braves had arrived that evening and didn't know what had gone on the last few days. They had come south, hoping wagon trains would be more plentiful in the south. Cochise had always been a hell raiser. Marques had tried to keep him in check, but now Marques and his son-in-law made a team.

"Marques Colorado Apache," Marcos called out.

More Indians were awakened by the shouting, so Marcos let them know. "Marques take wagon-train with plenty of loot." As proof, he threw his granite coffee pot on the ground and it made plenty of noise as the granite came off.

"Go in morning; get your share of loot." That would detain the braves for a while. They would rather have trade goods than fight John. Marcos rode in closer while he had their attention. "I have to water horse." They wanted to get to the canyon floor and follow the path along the stream. It was nearly impossible to travel next to the canyon wall because of the rugged terrain. Marcos guided his horse down the bank toward the stream as though there was no danger. Buck kept his mouth shut, but Amada put her hands over Buck's in fright. She had grown accustomed to life in the wilds, but about to escape, she didn't want anything to go wrong.

"You would be a fool not to get in on the trade goods; they even have fools water," which was a lie. Marques was too smart to allow his braves to have fool's water, but Cochise drank fool's water with his braves until they were in a stupor, then they lay down for a few hours to sleep.

They watered their animals and no one checked them out. Then they dismounted and walked close to the edge of the stream. The Indians were close enough to John that they would be taking potshots at him and his men in their bedrolls come morning. They probably knew where the Indians were and his vaqueros would be trigger happy at night and more dangerous than the Indians. When Buck was certain the guards knew someone was coming, he called out, "It's me, Buck."

They didn't return his call to come in, so they brought their horses to a halt and stood there waiting; the girl clung to Buck in fright. He only wished she were Suzy, but Buck didn't begrudge Amada her freedom. Suzy was out there, more vulnerable to the rigors of the wilds than the Mexican girl who had grown up little tamer than the Indians.

"It's me, Marcos and a girl." They all breathed easier.

"Put your guns down," Buck heard John say to the guards.

They walked in cautiously, but the vaqueros couldn't tell who they were and more were waking up and they had their guns at ready; they trusted no one at night.

"No white man would be wandering around these parts at night," someone shouted at them.

"A desperate man like Buck Garett would," Buck called back.

The metal of the shod horse struck the rocks along the creek bed, but the vaqueros were leery of Apaches with stolen horses and if Buck was captured, he could lead the lot to their destruction.

"It's me, John," Buck called out again.

"Buck, are you a hostage?"

"No, I'm not—but you're surrounded by Cochise's men."

"We know. That's why we're so cautious." John was no dummy. Even surrounded by Indians, he would outsmart them.

"Come in for better protection," John called back again. Buck was more than ready for the invitation. He led Prince in and Amada clung to him like he was her brave. If she were that afraid after a year, Buck wondered how Suzy felt—her little heart might beat itself to death.

"How did you ever get past the Apache?" John asked; he seemed worn. "The siege has gone on for too long a time."

"We are Apache," Buck said, flipping his clothing. "At least at night." It was dark enough that one couldn't see much.

By then the whole camp was awake and gathered around them. The vaqueros were especially interested in the girl Buck was going to marry.

"Is this the mail order bride?" John moved in close to look the girl over, while she pulled in back of Buck and away from the men. "This is Amada—the other girl is out there someplace in Apache camp. Come morning, I have to do something."

John and his men had been actually in reserve, picking off Indians from their stronghold to save the wagon train. But in the morning he expected to be hopelessly surrounded by Cochise's men.

"The fight is supposed to be over, but Marques has the supplies as well as the girl," Buck said. "You knew the same as I did, that Marques would not live up to his word."

"Come morning, the Cochise Apache will be gone," Buck said to John.

He was resigned, ready for battle. "How do you figure that?"

"Marcos told them they were getting beat out of their share of loot and there was aqua caliente."

"But the loot has already been distributed," someone shouted back.

"Anything to confuse the issue—then they'll be fighting among themselves."

"Or out of revenge they'll try and take the rest of the wagon train." John wasn't so dumb.

"That might be the most likely thing that could happen. The wagon train is out of water for the horses; a few have died. They have one man dipping all the time out of the hole they dug when it be safe. But that's not enough for all the animals." Buck told Nido to dig another hole in the side of the mountain where Prince had pawed at a wet spot.

"Come morning, I'll send two vaqueros over to the ranch to fill up some barrels." John must have been too sleepy to think.

"With the Apache in charge, we can't travel during the day." Then Buck fingered his drab clothing. "Not even with these duds—when I'm supposed to be Apache." Buck had on knee high moccasins and his face was splotched with yellow ochre. But Buck would have to depend on Marcos to talk.

When the vaqueros started to wander back to their bedrolls, Amada became less frightened. She found herself a blanket and fell asleep instantly. The vaqueros looked at her from time to time, but left her alone. Finally, only John, Marcos, two guards and Buck remained to hash out the events to come.

"A wagon load of water for so many animals won't do much good."

"You're right, John, but we have to save some of the animals."

"Eef we could get the best of the Indians—we could geet the horses to the arroyo where they could dreenk." Marcos could only think brute force.

"There are too many Indians; now we have Cochise men to fight. Buck figured if we had Suzy back—the only way they could win was to offer her service to doctor the kid. The only way the chief will hold off on more fighting."

"But we don't have the girl." John didn't have to remind Buck.

"With Cochise braves surrounding us—that's out of the question," John continued and pulled the blanket around his shoulders; it was getting late. A half moon was out and the night air had turned cool for that time of the year. Buck sat down, leaned against a boulder, and John followed suit. The two guards pulled further out to take their places for the rest of the night.

"Then we go now for water," Marcos said. Buck wondered where he got his strength. Buck was exhausted from lack of food and sleep.

"We'll load up with water from my brother's ranch early in the morning, get as close as we can to the wagon train and pull in tomorrow during the night." Buck knew they had to get going.

"Bring all the barrels you can," he said. "I'll make sure Jewell stays with Elena and the house." Someone had to protect the ranch, that's what all the fighting was about.

Prince followed Marcos' horse most of the way and where the terrain wasn't too rough, Buck nodded. It was nearly morning when he began to feel somewhat refreshed.

Long before they pulled into the yard, the dogs barked. The guard alerted the ranch hands and they were lined up overlooking the stockade, ready to greet their friends with an array of bullets. But when they determined it was Buck and Marcos, they came out of the enclosure and gathered round. They went inside the gate; even Elena was there carrying a rifle. Buck got down from Prince with Amada in his arms and Elena gave the two a big hug and asked how John was. "Fine!" John always comes out a winner. "This is Amada," he said, standing the girl on her feet. "She needs a home. She doesn't want a brave." Elena supported Amada as she listened to Buck.

Elena was a very affectionate woman; John was a very lucky man. "John has everything under control." Buck didn't have the heart to tell her he was surrounded by Cochise Apache. "We came for water."

The men scurried around and brought out a team and wagon. Buck told Elena, "Suzy be captured by the Apache."

Elena had been a prisoner for a time and knew. "How awful," she gasped. "I feel sorry for her and you, Buck."

"We have to get water to the wagon train and start looking for Suzy again."

"I will pray for her and for you, Buck." She looked at Buck with big round tearful eyes.

Buck turned away in bewilderment. No one had ever prayed for him, except his mother, and that had been so long ago.

"Well, if it will do any good." Buck couldn't think of any more to say. Jewell was coming with his gun and pulling his shirt over his head. Buck already knew what he had planned. When Jewell was even with the wagon, he said boisterously, "I'm going along."

"Like hell you are! You fill one barrel with clean water for drinking."

"Ah, hell!"

Elena went over and put her arms around him. "No cuss," she said. Buck guessed she knew better than to try and change his ways.

Jewell shook her loose. The dummy; Buck could have used a lot of that affection, if she hadn't been his brother's wife. That was the cause of all this commotion. But Jewell was too young to appreciate a good woman, so Elena went back to the house with Amada and fixed them some goods to eat.

Everyone worked silently, except Jewell. He grumbled while they bailed water from the stock tank. He was a grown man being treated like a kid, because he acted like a kid.

"Why did you wake me up in the middle of the night to carry water and now you won't take me along?"

"I didn't wake you up—you can go back to bed if you like. Besides, it's morning—you can see the red in the sky."

"You woke me up shouting and hollering and the dogs barking."

Buck didn't argue back, so Jewell started to shut up. John had fixed up a crude windmill and it was pumping a trickle of water into a horse tank and Jewell was catching it. Two men were dropping their buckets into a dug well closer to the house. The rest of them were dipping from the stock tank built of rocks, handing the water to two men in the wagon.

They were nearly ready to go when Elena brought out a huge basket of tortillas and jerked meat. If they ate all of that, they'd drink half the water by night.

Jewell stood at the back of the wagon and asked again. "I want to go along." He had the last bucket of water in his hand, swinging it. Buck was ready to climb into the driver's seat. Marco was mounted on a fresh horse and Buck had a new mount tied to the end gate of the wagon. Buck hated to leave Prince behind but he needed a rest.

Buck knew he had to be firm. "Look Jewell, I promised your pappy I wouldn't take you along."

"I'll take the blame—I'll tell Pa I talked you into it."

Elena said nothing. She had no real control over Jewell; she was only a stepmother, so she bid them bye and went into the house, and carried water to give Amada a bath.

Jewell climbed up and poured the last of his water into the drinking barrel; they didn't have time to look for covers for all the barrels, but knew some would splash out.

Jewell didn't want to climb down from the wagon; he was a good kid with a mind of his own. Buck climbed into the driver's seat and Jewell finally jumped to the ground. Buck called back to him and the cowhands, "Take good care of the place."

In the long run, as Buck said, Jewell's job was the most important of all. If the ranch were to be lost, everything would be lost. There had been a verbal agreement, hands off among the Apache after the trade for Elena, but it meant nothing. The Apache could overrun the ranch when John Garett was short handed.

Buck guessed Jewell had followed along on foot. When the team was down the trail a piece, he slipped into the wagon and in between the barrels. It was cool early in the morning and Jewell could stand the splashing water for no more than a mile. He worked his way to the front of the wagon and rose up to let Buck know he was there. "I couldn't wait; I wanted to see your new fiancée."

He knew Buck's fiancée had been captured by the Indians. Buck was half asleep and scarcely knew what Jewell was talking about. But Buck had a feeling it would be strange married to a girl about Jewell's age. Jewell hesitated before crawling into the seat with Buck until he noticed Buck was asleep. The reins were hanging loose; he grabbed them. It was easier than he had expected. The sun wasn't yet over the horizon when they hit a rut and Buck looked up sleepily at Jewell, glad he was along, but he had to say something.

"You have to go back, Jewell; I can't take you along."

He began to protest violently, "I can't walk all that way home. I'm a riding man. That would kill me." Then he laughed and Buck gave him a nudge.

"You're as wet as a dishrag."

Suddenly there was a vaquero out in front of them on the left side of the wagon and Marcos was on the right. Jewell pointed to the second vaquero. "I'm not the only one riding without permission."

Daylight came with a red sun against a hazy sky. This was going to be an easy day; Buck planned on getting some sleep when they holed up for the day, close enough so they could pull into the wagon train early at night. Then he would have to get back to looking for Suzy; without the red gown, she would look like any other Indian. They got the tortillas and jerked beef and had their fill of grub for the first time in days.

About the time they were enjoying the good meal, Buck was told, and John gave his vaqueros a pep talk and prepared for battle against the Cochise Apaches. The men scrounged around, eating what little food they had and drinking the last of their coffee. The rest depended on gut; they sneaked up the canyon, prepared to get rid of the Indians who hemmed them in, only to find them gone just like Marcos had said.

Some of the men said they had seen them go much earlier, but John wasn't too sure. They went back and gathered up their horses and blankets and decided to go up to protect the wagon train. They filled all their containers with water and followed a slanting trail out of the canyon, left by the Indians who had gone up and down the steep bank after water for ages.

With the Indians gone, it wouldn't be hard to get to the wagon train, even during the day John reasoned; he was in charge.

Just then, an arrow whizzed from the brush and buried itself in the chest of one of the vaqueros; he fell from his saddle. If he wasn't dead instantly, he was when he hit his head on the rock. When the Indian raised up to take another life, three bullets avenged the death of the vaquero. Before they got up the hill, they brought down four other of the Cochise tribe.

The vaqueros led their horses cautiously the rest of the way out of the canyon. When they could see the wagon train in the distance, they urged their mounts in that direction.

As they entered camp, Nido met them first, then the Frenchman came over. He was all in a dither about Suzy and asked about her. But Nido explained, "We think she might be out on the prairie by herself." Marques just sent a messenger saying, "Marques talk peace, bring Medicine Girl, fix Mito."

The news sounded good, but they didn't have the girl.

Frenchy was ready to look for her and make a deal. "No," John said, "Not yet." We'll deal, then look for her."

So John and Frenchy went to deal with Marques. The Medicine Girl would fix up his son if the Indians went home. The girl was indeed gone; they didn't tell Marques they didn't have her, but drove toward the ranch, after a promise that the camp would return to their Redlands to the north.

11

*B*uck wasn't much concerned about Jewell; he thought it was about time he grew up, but he would still have to explain to John why he was along.

Finally he said to Jewell, "What are you going to tell your pa?"

"I'll think of something." He didn't want to talk about it. "Look, you go to sleep. I'll drive."

Buck knew he wouldn't have trouble sleeping under any conditions. In fact he could sleep for days.

The dry land was dotted with sparse clumps of bunch grass and a sprinkle of chaparral. Jewell had the reins, surveying in the distance to avoid rocks and chuckholes. The seat was hard, but that was better than the wagon bed with the splashing water.

The wagon moved on for several miles, while the two vaqueros rode ahead prepared for danger, even though they were far from the hoard of warring Indians.

Then Marcos saw an Indian girl lying behind a clump of brush. At first it seemed to him that she might be dead. But when she moved to get out of the path of his horse, Marcos prepared to lasso her. Suddenly he let out a whoop of joy. At last he was going to capture himself a squaw.

Marcos called out to Buck, "What's this Apache squaw doing out here all by herself?" Buck was nearly asleep and couldn't be bothered.

Jewell answered Marcos, "The Apaches are everywhere."

"I'm going to have her for my squaw-wife." Marcos whirled the rope over his head several times, while the girl ran out into the open. He tossed the rope over her and started pulling her in.

"You must be desperate for a wife if you want an Indian," Jewell said from the driver's seat. He was rather unconcerned.

"I like Indians. I grew up with them for a time." Marcos wasn't watching the girl so she pulled the rope loose, then ran to get away from the path of the wagon. Marcos threw his lasso again and she came down in the dirt with a thud. Exhausted from traveling half the night, she lay there resigned to her fate.

Marcos climbed down from his horse and relaxed the hold of the rope so it wouldn't hurt her, but she started to free herself a second time, so he yanked her down. Then he picked her up in his arms, "Hey, this is a white girl."

"Probably one captured by the Indians." Jewell stopped the team. "Put her in the wagon, we'll take her along." She was so dirty and ragged he paid little attention to her.

Her hair was tangled and she looked wild-eyed as she squirmed in Marcos' arms.

He was a big brute of a man, but gentle as he lifted her over the end-gate of the wagon.

"Who are you?" Jewell started up the team. "You could die of thirst out here all by yourself. The water in the end barrel is fresh. There is a dipper on the bed of the wagon."

The girl disregarded the dipper, but grabbed hold of the barrel for support as the wagon bounced along. She put her face in the water and drank for a long while. When the ride proved to be too rough for her, she sat down, even though the water splashed on her from every which way.

Jewell stayed in the driver's seat handling the team and Buck beside him went to sleep. The fact that Marcos and Jewell spoke English didn't give the girl any real assurance. She was to the point where she didn't trust anyone.

Jewell began to look for a place where he could hole up until dark. They didn't dare get close to Marques Colorado and his marauding braves during the day.

But he had already gone too far.

The vaqueros were the first to spot the Apaches in the distance. They were Cochise men who had been fooled. All the booty had been taken and they were too few to take over the rest of the wagon train, composed of settlers.

They had gone back looking for John and his men, but they had joined the wagon train. They started in the direction of the Garett ranch. That was a ripe plum and their intentions were not honorable. Then they spotted Buck's wagon out on the flat lands. That wasn't much of a prize, but it would be easy to take, and they could avenge the loss of some of their braves. They came in riding hard, whooping it up, ready for the kill. There were perhaps fifteen or twenty of them. When Jewell saw the oncoming Indians, he secured the lines by fastening them to the seat and crawled between the barrels. He shouted to the team, sending them on in a gallop. The girl stood up to see what was happening and he pulled her down before leveling his rifle over the side of the wagon. It had double sideboards giving it higher protection. Jewell was young and craved excitement.

The vaqueros stopped the first two Indians when they were still out of range for their bows. That caused the rest of the Indians to veer off from the front of the wagon and drop back where they could slip up from the rear. Hidden behind the barrels, Jewel fired repeatedly, taking his toll of the pursuing Indians. "I need help," he called to Buck. But Buck slept on.

Jewell stooped down on the floor of the wagon, frantic while reloading his gun. "How did you get way our here all by yourself?" he asked the girl.

"I escaped from the Indians." She was dressed like an Indian, but her once pretty white skin was red from exposure to the sun.

The braves were close enough that Jewell used his revolver while the girl reloaded his gun. She said, "My name is Suzy Carver."

Knowing that Miss Carver was to be his uncle's wife, he couldn't help but reply, "Even though you look worn out, you are a lot prettier than I expected."

Suzy Carver looked at Jewell as though she had seen a ghost, and she liked what she saw. She had on a dirty shapeless dress that suggested an appealing figure, especially since it was splashed with water. "Your name must be Garett."

Jewell had his head over the end gate with his back to Suzy. "It sure is."

The arrows discharged by the Indians failed to find human flesh, but the wagon bed looked like a pin cushion. The Indians whooped and hollered and pulled in closer. Their loose hair billowed out as they dashed for the wagon. Some had braided hair that stuck out like pot handles. Jewell and the vaqueros took their toll as the team dashed out of control.

Buck had never been a winning man, but he could no longer say that. He supposed the Indians thought he was dead, slumped over motionless, or they would have put an arrow through him.

Suzy said to Jewell, "Then you must be the one who wrote the letter."

That was when Buck woke up and looked around. Suzy saw him and they recognized each other. Buck got off the seat and down between the barrels for protection. Suzy was over beside Jewell. Buck didn't know how she had gotten there. But he began to think, she thought Jewell was the one she was supposed to marry and she seemed right well pleased with him. Buck had to grant, he was young and handsome and was doing a real good job of fighting off the Indians, just like a professional.

Arrows were coming thick and fast; some stuck in the barrels, but none had penetrated the hard wood. Then one arrow whizzed by and sliced a large vein in Jewell's neck. He automatically dropped to the floor of the wagon. Buck saw the blood spurt forth and knew Jewell would bleed to death out in the wilderness. But Suzy automatically put her finger over wound to stop the flow of blood. She pushed him down on the floor of the wagon out of the way of flying arrows. Buck moved into Jewell's place and took his toll of close up Indians.

Jewell didn't see any more blood coming from the wound and started to get up. The girl pushed him back down. "I'll be all right." It all happened so suddenly that Jewell didn't think he was hurt badly.

Fortunately, the girl was a nurse. There probably wasn't another between the Garett ranch and Chicago. She seemed to know what to do as though she were brought up in the wilderness. "Hold still. A large vein is partially severed."

It might have been totally severed as far as Buck was concerned. He didn't think Jewell had a chance, nurse or no nurse. They had taken their toll among the Indians, so they veered off in the direction of Marques Colorado's permanent camp. Buck climbed into the driver's seat trying to slow the team, going at a dead run.

"Stop the wagon," Suzy called out. That took quite some doing, when they were going so fast.

Buck pulled on the lines, and yanked on the reins and pretty soon he had the team under control.

When the wagon was motionless, Suzy pulled a pin from her ragged apparel and bent over Jewell. Thinking he was the one she was supposed to marry, she was going to give him the best of treatment she knew how. She could have kissed him right then and there, but first she had to save his life.

"This is going to hurt. I'm going to pin that wound together."

By that time Jewell had come to the conclusion that he was indeed wounded and held still as commanded.

"Is it that bad?"

"I had just finished my nurse's training from that college in Chicago, when I put that ad in the paper and you answered it."

Jewell started to say something. Buck knew he didn't want to give her the wrong impression, but he was glad the way it turned out. Suzy shushed Jewell, "Hold still; don't move. Don't talk. I know this is going to hurt, but you have to hold still just the same."

Suzy wove the pin through the wound, partially stemming the flow of blood. "This is only temporary," she said as she continued to hold her finger over the wound to stop the leakage.

Jewell seemed happy, but bewildered that Suzy seemed to be interested in him. He wanted to be loyal to Buck, and looked in his direction where he was plugging a leak in one of the barrels. Buck picked up all the spent arrows, broke them in two and threw them out; the flint was sharp as broken glass.

Then Suzy called out, "I need a horse hair."

The remaining Indians found reinforcements and returned. Buck picked up his rifle. A horse hair at a time like this, but he supposed it was important. If he climbed out in front, he would be a target.

Buck didn't seem to move fast enough to please Suzy and she began to sound frantic. "I need the horse hair to stop the bleeding. I want to wrap it around the pin."

Buck looked in Jewell's direction wondering if he would live. He shouldn't have brought him along.

"Can you shoot a rifle?" he asked the girl.

"I'm a good shot with a revolver."

Buck liked the way she felt sure of herself after a couple of lessons with the Frenchman.

"Take this revolver while I climb out front and get you that horse hair." He hesitated to use Jewell's name. If he was going to turn the girl over to Jewell, Buck might have to do a little thinking.

Suzy still had her finger pressed against the gash on Jewell's neck. "The pin is in place, but there is leakage. Hold your finger over the wound while I try and cover for the man as he goes out on the tongue of the wagon." As Suzy lifted her finger from the wound, she placed one of Jewells fingers where hers had been. Blood oozed out and Jewell pressed harder to stop the leakage.

Buck's spirit sagged to a new low as he climbed out onto the tongue of the wagon.

"That's my Uncle Buck," Jewell said.

Why did he have to tell her, he thought as he climbed out of the wagon onto the tongue.

A look of determination spread over Suzy's face as she rested the rifle on the end-gate of the wagon, then she hesitated. But thinking of her capture, and how she was treated, she fired. The closest Indian, naked except for a loin cloth, twisted to the side, gave one last battle cry and fell from his horse.

The gun steadied on the bed of the wagon, magnified the report of the gun, causing the already frightened horses to start up with a jump, then on a dead run. Buck slipped and was straddle tongued, and jarred out of his wits. He steadied himself with one hand, and balanced himself the best he could. With one hand he righted himself. He plucked the hairs from the tail of one horse and climbed back into the wagon. He wove between the barrels and handed the hair to Suzy while the team dashed on.

12

*M*arques pointed to his son in the wagon. "Name Mito." Buck could tell he worried for the boy's life. That was an admirable trait; he was a changed man for the moment. He wanted something desperately, and would go through the humiliation of having the enemy restore his loved one's health. Many of his braves lay dead on the hot battlefield, but that wouldn't bother him as much as the loss of his son; perhaps, that was because he had lost his first son. He also had an older son who could replace the chief, but he preferred Mito. Even that was a step toward civilization. Showing compassion was not one of Marques' strong points nor of any Apache for that matter. Maybe they were making progress.

Suzy held her rifle over the side of the wagon; it could be raised, in an instant, the few inches necessary to center the chief's heart. "You can't make a deal with Marques Colorado." Suzy said it loud enough so the chief could hear. She looked at Buck as a wife might look at her husband, then she stared at Marques wondering how he would take the remark. He stared back, and since he didn't draw his lance, Buck supposed he tolerated her remark.

But Buck knew Marques felt hurt. He knew how the chief had treated the girl; he had expected her to wait for death patiently. But she lit out across the cactus, covered plains rather than face his verdict, death. If she was a Medicine Girl, she should have been there to help his people. The chief was a little addle-brained in his way of thinking.

Suzy was only quoting Buck when she said Marques couldn't be trusted. When Buck first said that, she thought he was being unreasonable and hard of heart. But after being captured, she held the same views as Buck did.

Now they had the ornery cuss over a barrel. If they didn't agree, he could turn his murderous horde loose on them, so they had no intention of taking advantage of him. In treating his son, they were only showing him mercy. Buck always maintained that someone had to show the Indians mercy the only way they could be taught mercy, the beginning of civilization in these here parts. Then they could live next to each other in peace.

"Things should be a might different this time, with the kid hurt," Buck said to the tired-looking girl standing there, still refusing to put her gun down. They had to have her cooperation or they would get nowhere.

As Buck began to bargain with Marques, John didn't say anything. Buck guessed he didn't have the heart knowing Jewell was hurt and he knew Buck had favored Jewell before and he would do it again.

"We'll take the boy to the ranch," Buck called to the chief. "Medicine Girl—from Chicago—great place of learning, she will fix Mito up." Buck was too proud to use the kid's name.

Marques' features were frozen into a perpetual frown; he didn't show the least sign of approval when Buck stooped to his way of thinking. But Buck supposed he would have smiled if he could have.

Suzy had never seen the young warrior before now. But without hesitation she said, "I'll fix the boy." She stood there facing the chief, looking as solemn as he, but she refused to use the kid's name, too.

"I'll do my part," Suzy said. "If the Great Spirit sees fit, He will do the healing."

"She wants you to understand—do not to expect a miracle." Buck tried to make the chief understand and he used the kid's name. Keeping the chief happy would be a small price to pay for peace. "Medicine Girl, fix up Mito." Suzy could have her pride; everyone has his or her faults, Buck included.

"You may make your home at ranch with Mito, but all braves must go back to their red land in the north." Colorado meant red in Mexican and the chief knew what Buck meant.

Buck climbed out of the wagon; the hot wind felt good flowing through his wet clothes. It would dry them out. Buck walked over to the wagon and looked at the young man, deemed valuable enough to bring this plundering to an end. He was lying on a number of blankets that Marques had captured in the exchange. Buck didn't know why, but somehow he felt sorry for the little cuss, lying there in pain and scared as hell.

John pulled his wagon in close to Buck's. Buck knew, on the uneven growth, every turn of the wheel jarred the young brave, and he could scarcely keep from whimpering. What a contrast from the night before when he was the idol of the young girls who ogled him from all sides.

"Right up close." Buck didn't have to tell John. Jewell was his son and he held his tongue, even though Jewell had gone counter to his orders.

"Sorry you're hurt, Jewell."

"I guess you were right Pa. I shouldn't have come."

"We won't talk about it—experience speaks for itself."

John got down to help Jewell into the other wagon. Buck climbed in first to move Mito over. "You're not the only one hurt around here." Mito moaned as Buck pulled a blanket out from under him and spread it out for Jewell.

With John's help, they got Jewell off the wet floor of the water wagon. Suzy was solicitous of his every move until they had him bedded down beside the Indian. Then Suzy sat down next to the boy and looked at his damaged shoulder while he stared back at her with beady black eyes, but for the life of him, he couldn't get up and run.

The bullet had gone through the top of his arm and then through his shoulder blade and out the back; there was no way Suzy could know the extent of the damage. His recovery would be long and painful.

Buck turned his wagon over to a mule skinner. "Take the water to the wagon train."

"They won't be needing it; by now they've driven the stock to the stream—the ones that could travel." Things were beginning to shape up. Marcos wanted to get back to the Garett ranch to make time with Amada; he began to hope he wouldn't have to lasso an Apache girl.

Then Suzy spoke to the Frenchman. "Better bring Bob over so I can take care of him."

"It's too late for Bob."

There was silence until Suzy said, "I'm sorry. Then, bring Dave over, so I can take care of his wounded leg."

The loss of Bob bothered Frenchy. Bob's sister was ailing mentally and he was afraid the loss of her brother might be the last straw.

"Bring my medical kit and my suitcase." Suzy sat there unashamed of her Indian clothes, or lack of clothes. When she bent over the Indian lad, it was hard to keep her breasts covered. With her dress they weren't supposed to be covered. That didn't affect Mito; Indian women didn't cover their breasts. But the worst was the effect of the sun on her delicate white skin; her arms and face were a mass of variegated red blotches. Suzy hadn't slept in thirty-six hours; she leaned back with a gasp against the side of the wagon next to her two charges. Marques, was mounted, ready to follow the wagon. But first, he rode over to his braves and made a heart-rending speech.

"I did not lead you to dishonor." He held his willow lance high for an instant, then he let its weight sag to the ground. He was a tired old man, but a good chief according to Apache standards. He hated to release his stewardship before his son Mito was ready to take over. In Buck's opinion, as far as the settlers were concerned, it was hard to believe there could be a worse ruler, but Buck knew his son-in-law Cochise was hell on two legs, especially when filled with fool's water.

He went on, "We have won many things to keep us warm through winter. Pack up your belongings and go back to the land of Colorado in peace." The old bastard sounded as though he really meant to have peace. "I will not return until Mito is well enough to travel north."

Buck knew it would be the Apache women who hitched the horses to tepee poles to be made into a shelter with animal skins. They would pile on their belongings and their children and head north. The braves would drive the spare horses and take side excursions to bring in game.

The Frenchman was ready to go back to the wagon train to reorganize; when his animals were strong enough, he would head east. But he had to pick up the plows left by the Indians, and sell what was left of them and his wine. If he picked up a few loads of hides to take back, the trip would not be an entire loss. Yet, he had nothing to look forward to except the arrival. He got down from his horse and stood beside Buck, next to the sick wagon. He held on for support as he spoke. "I promise myself, since I have nothing else, I weel take Suzy weeth me." Suzy had nearly drifted off to sleep, but when she heard what the Frenchman said, she bolted upright.

"I have something to say about that," Suzy shouted at the man.

"Wait a minute—I'm not asking Suzy to marry me, if she doesn't want to." Buck now knew she could have her pick of men. Jewell raised up for a gander, but his neck gave him a fit and he lay back down with a grimace and held still.

"She weel not want you—so we fight a duel eef necessary." Those were harsh words, but Buck was no coward. She was worth fighting for.

John was sitting there ready to move out; he stared at them but said nothing. Buck was anxious to see the wounded taken care of. It was a shock to Suzy as well as Buck and she screamed at the Frenchman, "I don't want any more blood shed."

Suzy climbed out of the wagon and stood there as though she were ready to take charge of a meeting. She wanted things settled peacefully; she wasn't used to a land without law that was ruled by the gun.

"Suzy weel be my wife—zen there weel be no duel," Frenchy announced so all could hear.

Buck couldn't help but admire Suzy; she was a spunky little chunk of beauty, even in her dirty rags. "I came to marry Buck Garett and I intend to do just that. He's just as brave and worthy of me as I expected. But he's too modest. He has encountered every danger imaginable to save me. That's not saying anything against you, Frenchy. You have done more than your part—for that I'm thankful and no more."

That made Buck feel right good, along with his clothes drying out in the hot wind. If Suzy wanted it that way that was the way it would be. The Frenchman thought high and mighty of himself and considered Buck a worn out nobody. He had expected Suzy to give in to his way of thinking, so he said nothing for the moment.

"If it's a matter of money," John spoke up. "We have several loads of hides you can have." John was ready to help. The Frenchman had given up his supplies for the girl, but in that there was love. Buck wasn't sure John understood that.

Du Lac mumbled something in French. Buck wasn't sure he wanted them to understand.

If it came to a duel, Buck had no intention of shooting a friend. Buck had never shot a friend. He had considered the Frenchman a friend, until now. And Buck wanted him as a friend again. This was a land of survival of the fittest, but for once Buck wouldn't fight back.

The matter was far from settled, one might say it was delayed so the wounded could be taken care of. Buck gave Suzy an assist as she climbed into the wagon. The scanty dress scarcely covered her pretty rump. The way the Frenchman fingered his gun, it seemed that he didn't want Buck to touch Suzy. But the Frenchman never shot on impulse like Buck did. He might think things over for several days before he shot. They parted without another word, not even a wave of the hands.

Buck drove the wounded in one wagon and John brought the water wagon back. Elena met them at the gate to the compound. Her first question was, "Where is John?" Buck pointed east to a little dot in the distance.

"He'll be bringing the water wagon back, M'am, and another Apache captive."

Elena took one look at Jewell lying helpless in the wagon, and screamed. There was little thought of the Indian for the moment, but if there was to be concern for him, it would come from Elena. She looked up at Marques in his yellow spotted shirt and little else. They recognized each other, but neither greeted the other.

Elena stood there befuddled, looking at Jewell.

Suzy spoke up, "He'll be all right, M'am." She jumped out of the wagon. "I'm Suzy Carter."

"I'm John's wife," she said to Suzy. "We will be sister-in-law."

"How nice." Suzy smiled and they gave each other a hug.

Amada was there wanting to do something helpful. Elena said to Suzy, "This is Amada, a captive of the Apache. She will assign you a room and help you get cleaned up while I see about Jewell."

They soon had Jewell in his room and bedded the Indian beside him. But Jewell objected. "He's too filthy. I don't want him any where near me—all covered with mud and blood." Jewell had a point there, but Buck intended to get a tub of water and wash him up. Marques followed around as though he didn't trust anyone. Buck said it was a good idea, just in case the boy didn't make it, they couldn't be blamed. He wanted to let the chief know that everything was on the up and up. Mito felt better when the chief was around and that too was important.

They then put Mito in the store room. There was no bed there and it was a mite dusty from crumbling walls, the only room where the walls had not been limed. But Buck was sure that Mito felt better with a cowhide on the floor and a blanket from the stolen goods. They threw a cowhide in one corner for Marques and he seemed pleased.

There was little Suzy could do for Jewell but wait and allow him to heal. But they cleaned Mito up and washed the mud out of his wounds. Buck held him down while Suzy poured turpentine in the bullet holes, both front and back. Marques was watching the entire procedure and was ready to slap the lad when he whimpered. All Marques knew was bravery. Suzy stood in the way when he raised his wrinkled hand. "No! No! Don't be so hard on him. He's hurt." The old bastard annoyed Suzy. But Buck, who had no authority over him, still didn't want him slapped around.

Elena put Suzy in the room between the sick, and Buck fetched her a tub of water and Amada brought some of Elena's home made soap and helped her bathe. The soap smelled like lye, but it removed some of the dead sunburned skin and sure got her clean.

After her bath Suzy slept for a couple of hours. When she stepped out into the dark hallways in one of Elena's black dresses, she looked somewhat rested. Buck went in to see how Jewell was doing; he didn't feel like talking. So he moved an old trunk over to the window and sat down with Jewell. Suzy went over and sat with him; she rested a hand in his. Buck had washed in the horse tank. Amada had jumped in and washed his back and they both felt clean for the first time in days.

It was nice having one so young and pretty looking up to him, but Buck couldn't help but say, "Suzy, I'm so much older than you. You don't have to marry me if you don't feel you should."

"But I will. I never go back on my word." She was young and sincere, but Buck didn't want an unmatched marriage.

Suzy put her arm around Buck. Jewell was watching, he raised up for a look, but the pin gave him what he deserved and he put his head back down.

"You will be my protector." Her eyes were so pretty when she looked up at Buck; at last he had found his place in the world.

"M'am, I always try and do the right thing. If I don't know what is right you tell me."

"I think you are right for me," she said, trying to be right jolly, as though they were no longer new to each other.

The thought of marrying Suzy no longer scared Buck. He began to believe they would make a right smart couple. Elena had given Suzy some cooking grease to put on her sunburned skin. It smelled awful, but it helped to ease the discomfort.

With a real needle and thread, Suzy was sewing up Jewell's wound, for the last time she hoped. "If this breaks loose too soon– you might be done for, so take it easy for a while. No horse back riding." Coming from Suzy, Jewell didn't object. But Buck knew, as soon as he could he would be out hunting deer and elk. Before he shot only rabbits; they were going to have more to eat than cow. Now that he was seasoned at Indian fighting, there would be no holding him back.

Buck handed Suzy a pair of scissors and she and she snipped a piece of jagged skin away a before making the next stitch. Suzy put another length of thread in the needle and looked at Buck for an instant as she put in the next stitch. "I'm going to have to learn to love you, Buck, but I will."

Buck knew it hadn't come at first sight, as it probably had with the Frenchman. But Buck understood. She was dedicated to her promises. As for Buck, he could never picture himself loving anyone but Elena. Maybe he was fooling himself, but he was still drawn to her; sometimes it hurt unmercifully.

Each time Suzy pulled the needle back a fraction of an inch, she put in another stitch. It was difficult for Jewell, but he wasn't in the pain the Indian was. Jewell was trying hard to be brave; his face scrunched up at times, but he held still and said nothing. He was a real Garett. Buck was right smart proud of him.

When John came into the room with Elena, she left out a sigh, "It's nice to have another woman around the house." She hung onto John's arm, glad to have him back.

John had been talking to the Frenchman and let him in on the news. "The wagon train is patching up their canvas. They have their animals turned loose on good grass along the canyon floor where there is plenty of water. The cow has already started to give milk again. With the scout dead, they needed someone to lead them to California. I'll tell you about Bob." Suzy took hold of herself at the mention of Bob.

"Have the Indians left yet?" Buck asked.

"They are on the trail going north, stretched out for about two miles."

Suzy stopped her work and turned to Buck then to John. "Please Mister Garett, I would like to hear the details about Bob, but after I finish here."

John turned around and glanced at Suzy; he wasn't used to being told when to be quiet.

"Oh, I'm sorry." Then he and Elena walked out of the room. Elena looked back and winked at Suzy and Buck. It did her good to have someone put her husband in his place.

Outside, John was dealing with the Frenchman. Buck had nothing to do with the sale of hides; they were John's hides. The less Buck had to do with the Frenchman the better; he might insist on his dumb idea of a duel.

Then Buck stepped outside into the sunlight. John called to Buck in a loud voice. "Come here, Buck. The hot headed Frenchman still wants to claim Lucy as his own."

Buck said, "I was hoping that he would go back east, to Kansas and hoe his grapes, without mentioning Suzy again." Buck was sure the Frenchman loved her. That was more than Buck could say for himself. Buck had a right to her. He would learn to love her, and would protect her and always respect her.

John and the Frenchman were talking idle about the hides again. "How much do you want?" and he looked at Buck.

"They are John's hides."

"You take them," John said. The stinking hides were already in the wagon. They should have made the deal first.

Buck was hoping things would go smoothly. Frenchy said in a surly voice to John, "That way you think you pay for the girl."

The hides were worth about a dollar each. So Buck said in a tone just as surly as the Frenchman was using. "How about two dollars each?" Buck thought that would put him in his place.

"After all you've been through, you deserve something," John said, still insisting on giving the hides to the Frenchman. That was being real friendly, but it didn't work that way.

"I'll come in about a week to take the girl. I pay for what I get. If you will not take money, I will bring a barrel of wine."

John and Buck looked at each other. They had never made a deal with anyone like the Frenchman. Suzy was resigned to marrying Buck; it was none of his damn business. Buck was annoyed at how abrupt the Frenchman could be. When Buck didn't agree at once to giving up the girl, he struck Buck a blow on the face with his stinking hand and Buck stumbled backward. Buck didn't want to fight; it was as though the man had gone crazy. Buck only thought to stay alive. He stumbled over some firewood and landed on his back. When Buck lifted up, he could have shot the man in the head, but he didn't.

"Ef you do not agree." He climbed nimbly on his horse, scowling at Buck with his large blue eyes. There was more than fire in them.

After wallowing in the dirt, Buck stood there erect, brushing the dirt off his back. He said with dignity. "On your return, I will have matters arranged."

Du Lac rode off holding his head high; dueling was a gentleman's way of dealing with disagreements. Buck had a week to mull things over; that would be hard on his nerves. Buck handled the hot tempered as they came along, always ready for a slash in the ribs. The Frenchman would duel for the girl; the new law said that was murder. "We best not tell the woman about this, maybe, we can wiggle out of it," Buck reasoned.

John grabbed Buck as they walked toward the house, "Maybe Cochise braves will take care of him."

Buck didn't wish the bastard any such luck. He wouldn't shoot the Frenchman. Suzy would never forgive him. "She maintains there has been enough killed, and she is right."

"You have a duty to defend yourself," John said.

Buck had never been a coward. Now that he had something to live for; he felt that the bottom had dropped out of life.

Later that day, Buck told Jewell what was happening. "She's worth fighting for," he said eagerly. "I'd fight a duel for her."

"If I kill the Frenchman, Suzy will not want to marry me." That set his nephew to thinking. Buck tried to look on the bright side. Frenchy was gone, maybe he wouldn't come back. He brought water for Suzy so she could wash the wounded and bandage them daily. She insisted on clean water directly from the well. No water from the horse tank where Buck bathed. He liked talking to Suzy, so he could get better acquainted with his betrothed.

Elena wasn't the same woman with Suzy in the house. She was always around as though she might be jealous of Buck. And there was Amada; she came into the house with Marcos to see Mito. They had seen each other in the Indian camp many times, but never really spoke to each other. But there was a difference. She was no longer the slave and she spoke a few words to Mito in Apache. Buck never really knew what she said, but she said it with a smile.

Soon Elena invited Amada and Marcos into the dining room and made coffee, so they could sit around and chat. Suzy was thankful to the girl she had changed clothes with. Amada's stomach stuck out, but she laughed about it and patted her midriff. "You were lucky you weren't around the Apache women to learn how few clothes they wore sometimes."

Suzy stared, round eyed and bewildered, thankful that she had escaped similar fates. Then she caught herself. She had retiring ways, but straight forward when need be. Suzy sagged into one of the high-backed chairs and Elena poured her a cup of coffee.

"Marcos is building us a one room adobe shelter," Amada said. Marcos got up and stood there awkwardly in his baggy trousers; his shirt had sleeves, expertly done since Amada now had a real needle. Marcos pulled on the rope holding up his baggy trousers. He was out of place with the women. He finished his coffee, and left to work on their one room adobe shelter. Then Amada popped up and rushed out to be with her man. The two seemed to agree on everything. Elena and Suzy sat there drinking their coffee. Buck came in and sat down next to Suzy.

"If Marcos decides to take Amada to the padre at del Bac to have the padre marry them, I was thinking the two of you could go along," Elena said

"How long will it take to get there and back?" Suzy looked at Buck for the answer.

"About a week."

"When the two patients get better." Her features were pleasant, as if she might be resigned and no more.

"I'll give you all the time you want if you really want to marry me, even though I am anxious since the matter seems to be settled between the two of us. I was thinking perhaps the Frenchman wouldn't insist on a duel if the two of us were married."

"It isn't going to bother Marcos and Amada if they don't get married. She is a little wild like the Indians. Marcos loves that. They will just live Indian style." Buck expressed his opinion.

"Is it safe to travel now? Are the Cochise braves still fighting us?" Elena asked.

"That they are, on a minor scale," Buck informed the two.

"We're going to have time to know each other better," Buck said to Suzy.

"I want to look pretty when I get married. Suzy was pulling on a piece of loose skin. Her face had started to peel. Even her hands and arms looked raw from the effects of the sun on her fair skin.

13

*S*hortly after the sun was up the next morning, Frenchy drove in with medical supplies for Suzy. Dave was along, riding his pony, because his leg bothered him less on the pony than the rough ride in a bouncy wagon. The two must have traveled all night—such dedication. But it was all because of Suzy.

Buck took Suzy the suitcase full of supplies and said, "I'll help you with the doctoring soon as I feed the Frenchman and Dave. They must be hungry. It might help to ease the tension between him and me. He fed me so I'll feed him." Suzy smiled at Buck and you could tell she was a bit uneasy with the whole situation.

There was always someone eating, so they sat down at the long table, rough planks nailed together, with three legged stools to sit on. Josh fried each of them several steaks and they had plenty of coffee and tortillas. That was the kind of food Buck liked along with beans. Frenchy's bread was better than the tortillas, but Josh, being Mexican was partial to tortillas, big tortillas, tough as leather when they dried out, but they stuck to your ribs.

After the first steak, the Frenchman patted his stomach. "I need a glass of wine." Buck poured him another cup of coffee. Dave agreed with Buck on the food, it was better than bread and wine. He drank four cups of coffee while they sat there, he with his leg stretched out. It didn't bother him much, but he tried to favor it as Suzy had suggested.

Just then Amada and Marcos came in. They looked happy together. She had on a new red dress and he had on a shirt of the same material, without sleeves; she was still working on the sleeves. Buck supposed the material had somehow been salvaged from the Frenchman's supplies. Amada was doing quite well, sewing with a needle Suzy had given her. Marcos had his bride at last, and Amada was happy, being treated as an equal instead of like a slave. She had dreaded the day when she would have become of a proper age, and six bucks might crowd into her tent to share her body.

Marcos and Amada sat across from Buck, and Amada got up to bring the food from the stove, built up with round stones and covered with a griddle. The wood fire was enclosed below. The room was already overheated and it was only early morning.

Marcos looked rested, but Buck would allow him time to finish his one room residence, and apply timbers as a roof. Then he would have to get off his duff and go back riding herd on cattle.

The mess room was a popular place early in the morning, the smell of coffee inviting. Marques came in. Buck didn't escort him around. He was on his own. If he didn't eat, that was his hard luck. Buck didn't want to have to look at his sour face any more than necessary.

Buck told the Frenchman that the vaqueros had gathered up another load of hides and would load them for him. He said he would have to help with the sick. He didn't say he would be helping Suzy; that could annoy Frenchy. Buck knew, according to their agreement with Marques, that Suzy had the responsibility of Mito. The Frenchman didn't ask to see Suzy, nor did Buck make any offer for him to see her this early in the morning.

As Buck got up he said to the chief, "We be going to bandage Mito, you better come and see." The chief didn't have anyone to braid his hair and it hung in sheets of long black and gray; he looked like a worn out medicine man.

When the chief came into the room, they already had Mito on his feet and the wounds exposed. Marques folded his arms and stood in a corner, watching every move, while they moved next to the window with their patient. Mito had his arm close to his chest, and Suzy had bandaged it that way. This time she drew the arm out to allow it to hang down. Mito screamed, but Suzy held his arm in that position. Marques was ready to step in and take charge, his hand lifted to strike Mito, but Suzy stood in the way.

His main thought was to have his son act like a brave. Buck had gotten tired of the way Marques was acting, but he supposed Suzy was handling the matter better than he could have. Buck could never have opposed the chief and gotten away with it the way Suzy did.

Suzy looked at the old man as though he was dirt under her feet, and Buck could see why. "From now on I have to change the position of his arm regularly so it won't grow back stiff and unusable. He is lucky he is in as good a shape as he is in." She continued her work and let Buck explain the best he could to the chief.

Buck showed the chief, "The holes are looking good. Suzy put some bought salve on them." Buck would never have used the precious salve; he would have used cooking grease. They bandaged the boy and bedded him down so he could rest and sleep as much as possible. Buck went over to the mess hall and brought back a steak with a rib for a handle and a tortilla. Mito took them gladly, but like the chief, there was never a word of thanks to anyone.

Jewell wasn't too bad off, but Suzy had to check the wound to make sure the artery was permanently closed so there was no leakage. She unwound the horsehair from around the pin. It had done its work but there was still a trickle of blood. As expected, Suzy placed a stitch at the end of the pin and pulled the pin back an eighth of an inch and put in another stitch.

Jewell sat there holding his head high. Then Suzy handed Buck the needle and unbuttoned Jewell's shirt and slipped it from his arm. Buck supposed it was modesty that prompted Jewell to say, "Do you have to take my shirt off."

"Yes," Suzy said. "I don't like the smell of it."

Jewell had had a bath, but he put the same shirt back on. Suzy's reply kept him quiet and let him know that he was but one step above the filthy Indian.

"The weather is warm enough that you need a clean shirt every day, but are lucky to get one once a week."

Suzy was clean and in a white uniform; she smelled pretty, just a faint odor of lye soap now and then. She hadn't taken time to put her hair up and it fluttered over Jewell's chest and over Buck's arms as he assisted her. It was soft and fluffy, all feminine. Buck was dressed as if he might be going to see Zulinda. He stood there holding a pan of water, with a towel over his arm. He handed Suzy a needle and thread as she needed it.

"Did you see enough action, Jewell?" Buck knew he had; he just wanted to say something.

"I sure did, Uncle Buck."

Suzy was all business. She held the needle up waiting for Jewell to hold still. There was a trickle of blood on her fingers; she dipped them in the pan of water and drew them across the towel. "If my stitching breaks loose, you could easily bleed to death, so just lie around for a few days until this heals up. No shooting an elk or deer, not even a rabbit."

Buck handed Suzy a scissors and she snipped away jagged pieces of thread before putting in the next stitch.

It was refreshing to have Suzy around the house. Then she turned her back as she worked. She thought again that she was

going to have to learn to love Buck, because she wasn't going to go
back on her word.

14

It was Elena's influence that changed the store-room into a sick room, but mostly Buck's labor. The dust flew as Buck brushed the adobe walls down, so Suzy took Mito for a walk. He looked with amazement at Marcos as he laid up the adobe blocks on his half-built room.

While Buck painted the walls of the sick room with lime, the boy watched him with half-closed eye. By the time Buck was at the wall where Mito was resting, he was glad to move. The walls turned a dull white until they dried, then they turned bright and cheerful. Eventually Marques ventured a complimentary, "Nice."

When the walls were thoroughly dry, Elena hung curtains over the lone window and tied them back to let in light, but closed them during the heat of the day.

The old chief came regularly to visit his son, and lay in a dark corner where he scowled at anyone who came around. The two looked at each other, but scarcely ever spoke a word. Buck knew then that the kid was still in pain when he moved. Yet he was more like a wild animal than a human being; he would have to behave himself for a while. He avoided the English language like Buck would avoid a plague.

When the future chief's shoulder stopped hurting, he started to walk around. He and Jewell were thrown together. If they hit it off well, they could avoid future wars and save a lot of bloodshed.

Then Suzy changed the boy's routine. Buck was not in the room at the time of the first session, but she stood him up and tried to explain. "You have to exercise your arm." She removed the sling that held his arm in place. She helped him lift his arm and hold it out straight. The pain was excruciating and he screamed, "You are killing me," the only English he seemed to have learned up too that time.

Marques was always near when anything was done for his son. Buck tried to make sure of that, since he had no trust in anyone; Buck was trying to build some. That time Marques was lurking in the dark hall that connected with all the rooms. When he heard the scream, he rushed in and found that Mito was only asked to lower and raise his arm. That seemed a simple matter to him and he slapped the boy on the face. The kid grabbed his arm and Suzy without thinking, slapped the chief, then she ordered him out of the room. "Don't you ever come back in this room again."

The chief staggered out of the room as fast as his old legs could carry him. Suzy had spunk. That was the girl Buck was supposed to marry. She could be brave on a one-to-one basis, when the chief wasn't surrounded by an army of braves.

Since Buck was not in the room at the time, Suzy came looking for him. Buck was polishing a saddle for Suzy. "The saddle is for you."

That was the farthest thing on her mind at the time. "I slapped Marques," she confessed. Then she grabbed hold of Buck like a bad child wanting approval.

"You probably did the right thing. If I slapped him that would be like declaring war; there would be a lot of minor scuffles with his braves." She loved Buck for his opinion. Buck allowed the old crank no weapons, so Buck carried none, hoping to build up a bond between the two of them.

Marques had had his way long enough; he had gotten all the supplies belonging to the Frenchman. He was having his son cared for by the enemy, but the final settlement was not over with yet, especially if they angered him.

Marques felt lost, wandering around the compound and started to build himself a wickiup. There was scarcely anything to work with, but a meager supply of firewood. Marcos was there with Amada, the two lying in the sun instead of making more adobe blocks. Buck allowed him to make his own shelter, but he would soon be back on his horse again.

Amada, even though she had been one of the chief's subjects, refused to talk to him as she did to Mito. He would have to get rid of the spoils of war, when it went against him. But Marcos took pity on the old man, setting up a few willows and having no hides to cover the framework.

Marques and Marcos parleyed back and forth until Marcos hitched a team of horses to a wagon and he and the chief went to a stream and brought back enough willows to build the tepee and some poles to cover part of the roof when Marcos got that far on the building.

That afternoon Marcos and the chief completed the tepee and Marques crawled in to be out of the sun and lay down on the bare earth. Buck was sure Marques would feel better there than in the adobe structure. No matter that it was cool inside the big house, Marques wasn't used to comfort.

Buck was beginning to get restless working around the house, especially for two Indians who had tried to kill him just a week ago. Sometimes it kept Buck away from Suzy; he wasn't sure but Elena had planned it that way. Buck belonged on a horse. He wasn't born to ride; he had grown to the habit. He groomed and curried a fine filly for Suzy. She couldn't go on caring for the sick forever. Taking care of the sick was one thing, but she had to get away from that, and back in the wide-open spaces. Buck saddled Prince and the filly and led them up to the door. Jewell was walking around and he asked Suzy to come out. She stood there beaming as though she had not come west to find a husband, but to learn to ride a horse. Buck could tell Jewell wanted to come along. It took but a minute to look at the scab on his neck. The wound was no longer bandaged, but Suzy had removed only half the stitches.

Suzy shook her head. "One week more," she said to Jewell. He kicked the dirt, but didn't pout. Buck knew he was lost on foot, the same as he was, but Buck didn't want him along anyhow.

Luckily, Suzy had her hair done up in a bun so it didn't blow about. Her dress worked up to show her legs; they weren't sunburned much. "We'll be getting you some material for a riding habit."

"Oh good, I guess I need it." She and Buck looked at her legs and smiled. She wasn't the least bit shy. She appreciated being feminine, the same as Buck appreciated it. She had a wide brim Mexican hat on her head, with a leather strap under her chin that would keep off the sun until she got used to it. Soon, she would be as brown as a coffee bean and you wouldn't be able to tell her from the Mexicans except by her blond hair. They splashed across a tiny stream where some of their cattle watered. The horses took time to drink and they had time to look at the grassy valley. "We try to winter some of our cattle here, but it's difficult to keep them away in the summer."

The third day out they took two containers of water and a packed a lunch. Suzy's nursing responsibilities were coming to an end. Jewell had only to be careful not to tear the wound open by accident. Mito walked around with his arm in a sling, so he could favor it. He loved the mess room and ate like a horse.

They ventured farther out each day. Elena loaned Suzy her

riding breeches, fringed with leather straps, so she didn't have to show her bare legs and rub them raw.

On one of the rides, they were getting ready to dismount and sit in the shade of a clump of bushes when they saw someone resting under a meager bush ahead. Shade was scarce on the grassy bottom and they saw the feet before they saw the man. Buck wandered if someone had been killed by the renegade Apache. He didn't know they had gotten this far in their direction. As they approached, the bare feet looked red and swollen. Then Buck saw it was the Frenchman. He had been without food or water for at least two days and the stream was but a short distance away. Buck got down and gave him a drink from his container. After he had taken several drinks, they offered him food. He didn't like eating, even though he was weak. He had been delivering the barrel of wine.

"Zee Apache kill my man. Zey take my wagon, my wine, my water, my gun, my boots and cut the bottom of my feet."

Frenchy had been coming to deliver the barrel of wine to the Garetts when the renegade Cochise braves killed his mule skinner, but not Frenchy. They thought he would die a more miserable death without boots or water and not being able to walk.

Buck didn't mind them taking his gun; he was probably going to use that to fight the duel. "Did they get Dave?" Suzy asked.

"No, they did not get Dave. Dave get well and not come along."

That was a big blessing as far as Suzy was concerned.

When Frenchy felt a little better, Buck helped him onto Prince and they took a fast clip toward home. When Buck didn't trust someone, he always put them in front. That was where he put the Frenchman, even though he didn't at that moment feel he could cause any devilment. They crossed the valley of lush grass and a number of elk on the far side of the stream looked up in their direction before they ran.

When Prince grew tired of the added weight, he dropped

behind the filly and took a slower clip toward home and the watering tank.

Buck couldn't help but needle the Frenchman, the man who wanted to fight a duel. He suggested, as soon as they got to the house, that they both fight barefoot using willow poles. Buck knew he couldn't walk a step with cut feet, so he gloated. That was mean of Buck, but he did want to squelch the duel, once and for all.

Frenchy refused to reply for a long while. Finally he muttered, "When I get well, zen we fight."

Then Buck knew he would never give up the silly idea of a duel.

There was little they could do for the Frenchman but feed him and put him down in the bunkhouse where he could rest. Suzy bandaged his feet.

Buck slept in the bunkhouse. He didn't intend to sleep in the house until he and Suzy got married, so Frenchy couldn't say he was playing favorites.

They were determined to track down the renegade Indians come morning. Jewell didn't mention coming along this time. Buck was sure he would have, but he was still under Suzy's orders, be careful.

The next morning, while Elena and Suzy were still asleep, John and Buck climbed the ladder to get onto the roof, to look over the countryside. "We might have to tie that rung back on," John said. They had gone up the ladder a hundred times and had forgotten that one rung was missing. But John was owner of the ranch and it was his business to keep things in repair. Buck followed up the ladder; they did need a new rung.

They stood there in the fresh air. Morning was a wonderful time of the day, before the blinding sun was out. "There's a future in this land," John said like a real brother. "And I am happy you'll be a real part of it, Buck. She's pretty, Buck. I must say you deserve a good woman. And I must say that you earned her."

"I allow you are right."

The sun was peeking over the horizon. Ferd was there on the dirt roof, curled up in his ample serape.

"Go down and get yourself a cup of coffee and a steak," John said to Ferd as he looked up. "We won't be needing a guard up here when peace comes to our land," John commented, knowing Ferd had been asleep.

"With Frenchy's wine, Cochise braves are always drunk, and being picked off one at a time when they get into a scuffle," John commented as Buck scanned the desert surroundings. It was pretty and pleasant before the heat turned the atmosphere into a dull haze.

Down below, a rooster crowed. The battle with the Indians hadn't affected the chickens; they were up and around scratching in the dirt for bugs.

John stood up straight. He was a big man. He crowed just like the rooster. "Cock-a-doodle -do." Buck couldn't help but laugh. John was happy. He didn't blame Buck for Jewell getting it in the neck. He would soon be on a horse where he belonged. There was nothing to the north or west, then he turned his scope to the east. In the distance was Frenchy's wagon with a number of Indians around it. Buck supposed they were all drunk.

"We are going to be one big happy family," John assured Buck. Buck then knew where the Cochise bucks were. If they are drunk, they will be an easy mark.

Buck wasn't watching the Indians close up, that was the farthest thing on his mind. He had his back to the palisades where the Cochise braves were hiding. A shot rang out and nicked Buck's arm. John stopped clowning and stopped to see if Buck was hurt. When he saw it was only a scratch he turned to see where the shot came from. He grabbed Ferd's gun. The Indians were already climbing over the enclosure, ready to jump inside. The vaqueros were in the mess room waiting for John and Buck to move out. John took the Indian with the first shot and he tumbled back, screaming, "Marques, Marques."

Then came the blood curdling cries from the other side of the fence, "Marques, Marques."

Buck thought they were mad because they were holding their chief a prisoner. The Indians had their ponies hidden in the depression from banking the dirt up inside the fence. They mounted their ponies and headed for the wagon and the barrel of wine. Buck counted seven while favoring his arm. It was bleeding enough that he had to hold his finger over the wound.

They had gone onto the roof unarmed; John hurried down the ladder with Ferd's rifle. The vaqueros were mounted and waiting for a leader. That was generally Buck's job. But John jumped astride a horse and led the group out to the gate, where Buck pulled it open. The braves were already a mile away, but they gouged their horses in hot pursuit.

Then a shot rang out and John fell from his horse. Buck was of little use since he hadn't been carrying his gun because of Marques and the Frenchman. By that time Marcos was at Buck's side and neither were armed. They rushed out and stood before a wounded Indian. Marcos kicked him in the neck, but John died before the Indian did.

When the vaqueros saw that their leader was dead and Buck's arm was covered with blood, Marcos took the lead. With fresh horses the vaqueros were able to catch up with the Indians and picked off several. They chased the others far enough away that Buck said when they sobered up they would never come back. The vaqueros didn't get back until nearly evening, but they brought the wagon and a nearly empty barrel of wine. Written on the barrel was something that Buck couldn't read, "Ces tunneau du vin payera pour la fille." Buck told Suzy about it; the next morning she went out to read the message.

"This barrel of wine will pay for the girl." Before, Buck didn't know how precious she really was.

They buried John next to Maryanne. Buck led Elena by the arm and Suzy held onto Buck's wounded arm. Jewell lagged behind and the Frenchman limped along with the vaqueros. They sat around the living room for several days drinking coffee and brooding over John's death. Elena got one feeling out of her system. "So many people get killed." She wasn't thinking just of John. It didn't bother Buck in the least if a few Indians got killed. He was used to that, but it shook him up when John caught lead. Buck said it should have been him; John was a better man than he.

"All those Indians buried out there. It was as though they never lived," Elena moaned. They were more human to Elena than to Buck, because she had lived with them.

Suzy took it all in her stride, she hung onto Buck from time to time, but she never went outside. She wanted to stay away from the Frenchman, but went there anyway and wound his feet with white linen from his supplies. "I think you are worth more than a barrel of wine," Buck commented time and again to Suzy.

She smiled up at Buck. "But it's such good wine. We have no salads, so the acid helps to digest our food." The nurse had studied better eating habits.

"I guess, you can't put a price on his wine any more than we can put a price on you," Buck said to Suzy. Buck hated to build the Frenchman up. He thought his intentions were good, but he refused to tell him so.

Frenchy was hobbling around the compound in a pair of soft Indian moccasins. Then Buck discovered he had a revolver attached to his waist and was practicing the draw in back of the barn. Buck knew the Indians had taken two weapons from him; he didn't dare tell Suzy, but he told Jewell.

Jewell was always walking around the compound looking lost. He helped Marcos put the willows on his roof. He eyed Amada from time to time. But mostly, he waited for the day when he could ride and shoot a deer. Really, he was trying to do what was sensible, because he no longer had a father to tell him what to do, or what not to do.

Buck approached Jewell. "The Frenchman still wants to fight

a duel with me, for Suzy, he's real serious."

"I tell you, she is worth fighting for, Uncle Buck," he lashed out excitedly.

"I know, I know, but I don't want to shoot the troublemaker."

"Why don't you put a pistol on and keep an eye on the man?" Jewell seemed so anxious, that Buck began to think that he might have made a mistake asking Jewell.

Buck met Elena in the dark hallway. She looked so tired; she put her hand on his shoulder as if to keep from falling. He thought he might be free from his longing for her. But he wasn't prepared for how he felt when she rested her hand in his. He knew then that he would never be able to turn her loose.

The Indian had now moved out of the house and into the tepee with the chief and father.

Suzy told him, if he could hold his arm out for two minutes, she would be ready to turn him loose. He was as anxious to leave as she was to get rid of him. He no longer had that hang dog look of a wild animal. He trusted the people at the ranch and walked around the compound as if he might build something like Marcos' shack when he got back home. But that meant he would have to live in the same place continually.

It was taking the compound a long while to settle back to normal after John's death.

Elena was especially in a dither, but she worked in her garden early in the morning while it was still cool. She sometimes stood there leaning on the hoe thinking; her head covered with a large brimmed Mexican hat. Buck was supposed to carry water. He wanted to assign one of the vaqueros, but Elena didn't like the idea.

"You bring this wonderful girl back—Buck, I am happy for you. Good it is how it all turned out for you, but so many deaths, and now my husband."

Buck didn't tell her he was going to have to fight a duel with the Frenchman; then there would be another death.

Meanwhile, unknown to Buck, Jewell didn't mess around. He

poked his gun into the Frenchman's ribs and lifted his revolver from its holster.

After Jewell disarmed the Frenchman, he took one of the Garett horses and headed for his outfit. Buck hoped that would be the last he would see of the man. But Jewell said he would be back, so he stayed on the alert.

And, sure enough, two days later the Frenchman was back with a fancy weapon fastened to his side.

The gate to the compound was already closed when he arrived late at night. So they let him sleep out in the open. Jewell was ready to shoot him, but Buck wouldn't allow that, even though, Buck knew he had come for no other reason than to fight a duel.

When Buck could no longer ignore the situation, he went out unarmed while the Frenchman fingered his new weapon, as if he couldn't wait any longer to shoot his enemy.

Frenchy climbed on his horse, so he could look over the gate. "Get your weapon," he shouted at Buck.

Dave was there; he was supposed to be Frenchy's second. He rode over where he could talk to Buck through the fence. "I don't like this anymore than you do, Buck. You have my permission to shoot him. I have always been loyal to the Frenchman, but I can hardly abide by what he is trying to do now."

Buck's left arm was still bandaged, but he could fight with his right arm, so that would scarcely keep him from fighting a duel, if he really wanted to fight.

Then Elena stomped out the front door. She knew the Frenchman had come for Suzy one last time. "Stop. None of us want a duel," she said to the Frenchman.

Jewell came out of the house acting like an officer of the law. "Leave your weapon in the saddlebag or we won't open the gate."

"Don't take his weapon this time," Buck said to Jewell.

"I don't want you kilt, Uncle Buck."

"We're all going to go inside right now and hear what Elena has to say. After that we will play it by ear," Buck said.

Elena seated the Frenchman at the dining room table and Buck across from him, and they scowled at each other. Suzy walked around grimly and poured each a cup of coffee. Then she came back and put her hands on the back of Buck's chair. He took hold of her fingers hoping to give her assurance.

Buck spoke up first. "I have decided," he spoke as if he had the right to speak for everyone present. "The wagon train is about ready to leave for California. I will lead them." He stopped to let that soak in. "There is no one to guide the helpless creatures; if someone doesn't lead the poor devils, they will go nowhere except to their death. I have been to the coast; it is still more than eleven hundred thirsty, winding miles, most of it through the hot desert. The best time to cross the desert is in winter."

"Uncle Buck, if you go to California, I'm going along," Jewell spoke up.

"I won't take you along, unless you promise never to hunt alone." Jewell looked as if he might be thinking.

Everyone listened—each wondering how, he or she would fit into Buck's unexpected plan. The Frenchman's eyes looked restless; Suzy was resigned to the fact that the settlers had to be saved. "I will follow the same trail that Colonel Cook used. It went winding as far south as Mexico. The only trouble he had was when he was attacked by Mexican fighting bulls. He lost a few horses and one man," Buck said.

"Now wait a minute," Elena finally spoke. "You can't run away from Suzy." Then she sat down to think.

"I deplore all the deaths, especially when the people are young, even that of the Indians. I may not want Buck to go, but I am sure that the settlers need him," Suzy said.

It was then that Elena got up and took Suzy into the parlor. They were gone for a long while and the Frenchman stared at Buck with hate in his eyes.

Finally he said, "When Bob died, it was not like one of the Indians buried out in the hot desert. He had a sister who promised to miss him. I have to bring someone home to replace her brother."

He was begging Buck for the hand of Suzy. Buck liked that better than shooting it out.

Then Elena and Suzy came back into the room. Elena looked delighted. Suzy somewhat bewildered. She allowed Elena to do all the talking.

"When Buck gets back from California, he can marry me if he wants. He always wanted to marry me, but he has been too shy."

Elena put her cards on the table. "I didn't have to say this, but I don't think anyone is going to be unhappy, especially the Frenchman." But when Buck looked over at Suzy she seemed very solemn and started to cry. She had said to Buck that she wouldn't marry him if he fought the duel. She didn't say that about the Frenchman. Buck supposed he was only expressing love, in his odd way.

Buck got up to take Suzy by the arm to express his feelings. "You don't have to go along with Elena's suggestion."

"I think it's a very sensible solution, it's just that I got to loving you. I just have to get used to it. It won't be too hard; Elena has been preparing me for days." She looked over to Elena accusingly as she stood there out of place.

Frenchy heard Suzy sniffling and stood up. His feet were well, but he still wore the soft skinned moccasins. He shuffled over to Suzy. She put her head on his shoulder and lost a few tears of resignation. Suzy didn't say it was better this way, but the Frenchman would have insisted on a duel and Buck would have been at his mercy since he refused to shoot the man.

Buck would have to adjust how he now felt about Elena. When he got back from California in about eight months, then they could mosey over to Mission San Xavier del Bac and the priest would tie them up permanently.

||||||||||||||||||||||||||||||||||||

www.ingramcontent.com/pod-product-compliance
Lightning Source LLC
Chambersburg PA
CBHW011739010726
47496CB00010B/2997

* 9 7 8 0 8 6 5 3 4 7 1 8 2 *